A KISS IN THE DARK

ALSO BY JANA L. PERKINS

A KISS IN THE DARK

JANA L. PERKINS

Copyright © 2025 by Jana L. Perkins

First edition, 2025

ISBN 979-8-218-59263-9

❀ Created with Vellum

Dedicated to those who have had love take them by surprise

CHAPTER 1

EDWARD LIVINGSTON

BATH, ENGLAND
JANUARY 2, 1817

It was my preferred place to be: the dark. I never was one for parties, especially balls. They always left me with a headache. To make matters worse, the new year had just been ushered in, and Bath was holding its first public ball of 1817 now that the bell ringing had ceased and all superstitious traditions and nonsense alike had concluded. It meant, however, that this particular ball was a crush, bringing anyone and everyone. Mrs. Hale had been lecturing me not five minutes ago about my severe expression, stating that I lacked equanimity.

"Really, Mr. Livingston, you should ask one of these fine young ladies to dance," the nosy woman had said as she raised her inquisitive grey eyebrows. "I don't believe even *you* can deny the abundance of beauty before you, and though you can't claim to be as handsome as some gentlemen, I daresay your dark curls and blue eyes are enough to tempt most young ladies."

I pressed my mouth in a firm line, annoyed. "Their beauty I cannot deny," I said curtly. "And yet they still don't interest me."

"Oh, pish." She swatted the air. "You may just have to thaw the ice around your heart. I daresay a woman's touch would do you good." She then continued to point out every lady in the room, relating to me her connections, status in society, wealth, and any ramblings she thought I would find useful.

She was still prattling when I turned and walked out of the ballroom. Now, reclined on a settee in the blackness of a secluded room, I massaged my temples and was grateful for the coldness of the quiet space. I would return to the festivities after a good nap.

My thoughts wandered to Mrs. Hale's words. My problem wasn't so much an icy heart as a straightforward mind. I was logical. Why would a pretty face make me feel something? Ever since I'd been snubbed by Katherine Baker when I was 17, I'd been determined not to succumb to such reckless compulsions. It wasn't that I didn't enjoy beauty, but it did nothing for me. True, I hadn't danced with or spoken to a woman unless we were in a group for a number of years. I simply observed them from afar. And no, I wasn't intimidated, I reassured myself. How different could dancing with a woman really be from acknowledging her beauty from across the room? I answered my question as I so often did:

It would be exactly the same.

Precisely.

A beam of light interrupted my thoughts. The outline of a dress swept inside, then just as quickly as the door opened, it clicked shut once more, and blackness returned. Light footsteps moved in my direction. I stood up quickly and opened my mouth to make my presence known when a hushed feminine voice penetrated the darkness first.

"I was afraid you might not come," she breathed. Her voice shook slightly as if she was anxious.

Confused, I paused. I searched for something to say . . . anything. My heart certainly wasn't picking up speed at her unexpected entrance. At least that's what I told myself. And why was it suddenly so blasted hot in this room when it had been cool mere seconds ago? I opened my mouth once again to state that I was leaving, but her hand found mine before the words came out, making my mind go completely blank. Her fingers were soft and delicate. They were cold and soothing against my skin, which was now blazing like an inferno. Where were her gloves? If only I could see who she was.

I went rigid as her fingers wrapped tenderly around my wrist. She exhaled slowly as if the simple touch alone was a balm, then stepped closer and brought her other hand to rest in mine, the fabric of her dress rustling against my knees.

An odd leaping sensation formed in my stomach, resulting once again in a lapse of judgment—I was completely incompetent at forming a single word. My pulse raced as her hands gently moved up my arms and then onward to my shoulders. My breath picked up speed when she laced her fingers behind my neck. A light floral scent met my senses as she leaned into me and gingerly pulled my face towards hers. Soft lips brushed against mine. My heart pounded fiercely. What was happening? And why wasn't I stopping it? I found myself under some kind of spell, holding perfectly still.

When I didn't reciprocate her kiss, she pulled her head back in what felt like surprise, and her fingers released me. The coldness of the room suddenly returned, this time uninviting.

"Will you not kiss me?" She sounded surprised, as if this was an ordinary greeting. "My uncle says he will send me away in three days if he doesn't kill me first. We are running out of time." She took a small step back, most likely trying to see my expression in the darkness with as little luck as I was having seeing hers. My brain finally registered a part of her words. Was her comment about her uncle killing her in jest? The way one would state their wish to be rid of someone? Or was the comment in earnest?

My perfectly logical brain finally took over and found the words I should have uttered from the very beginning. I would take a step backward and calmly say, 'Madam, clearly you have mistaken me for another man.'

Except, instead of taking a step backward, I stepped forward. And instead of saying those simple, honest words, I found my arms moving around her waist.

She breathed out slowly in relief and let her arms rest on my chest.

Why did I do it? I can't *logically* say, other than the fact that it felt right to have her there. As if she belonged in my arms. But I pretended it was simply to prove my theory that holding a woman would feel the exact same as looking at her from across the room.

I couldn't have been more wrong.

She felt wonderful, whoever she was, leaning into me. I pulled her closer, not knowing why I did it or what would happen when she realized I wasn't the man she believed me to be.

"What are we to do?" she whispered.

I certainly couldn't speak now. Not after she'd kissed me and I had her enveloped in my arms. If I whispered quietly enough she most likely wouldn't be able to detect the difference between my voice and—his. I could tell her to meet me here in an hour, then walk away. Then she could meet the gentleman she believed me to be later, and they could continue this conversation. Logically, it was a perfect plan.

But realistically, I was loath to let her go. She fit so perfectly right where she was. I suddenly had the bizarre desire to be the man she held affection for. I told myself it was ridiculous. But there was something about the way she opened herself to me . . . or, I supposed, this other man. She trusted me—him. I felt it in the way she breathed and held tight to me. I wanted to know who she was; what was inside her mind, her heart; how long she had loved—him. Her kiss had been pure and sweet.

I continued to hold her with one arm while my other moved upward in the darkness. If I would never know who she was or what she even looked like, I wanted to discover as much as I reasonably could. My fingers brushed against her neck as I tried to find her face. Her soft skin sent small currents of electricity throughout me. My fingers then moved up along the curve of her jaw and to her cheek. I should have stopped there, but my fingers drifted down slowly until they brushed her lips. I felt her smile beneath my touch.

"Are you memorizing me?" she teased. My heart skidded at the sound of her lightly flirtatious tone. Oh, she was lovely. Her accent was refined, her voice kind and melodic. On top of it, she wasn't talking about the number of couples in the ballroom, or the general splendor. She wasn't gossiping about the latest scandal. She simply wanted three more days with me—well, *him*—until her uncle sent her away, the blackguard.

Each second that passed with this mystery woman was another second she was more likely to discover my identity. And each moment that I felt her heart beat against mine as I wrapped my arms tighter about her, or heard her exhale with satisfaction at being near me, I became more pulled in by her very existence.

"You are being very mysterious not speaking to me." I could hear the smile in her voice. "Very well, I will memorize you too."

I held perfectly still and closed my eyes as her fingers moved over my face. It took everything in me not to take her hand and press her slender fingers against my lips.

It was time for me to take my leave. I inched my face forward, brushing my cheek against hers until I was close to her ear. I parted my lips to speak the hushed words that I had played over in my head, *come find me later,* but they were caught in my throat. Could I really just leave without knowing who she was? She waited for a moment, then turned her lips toward mine. Her breath came out in soft whispers against my cheek. It felt as though she was waiting for me to kiss her.

My heart pounded as I considered what to do. I turned my lips towards hers, now only a breath apart, to see if she did in fact want to kiss me again.

It was the last thing I thought before she closed the distance. Our lips moved slowly against each other, and her fingers caressed the side of my face. They then slowly moved to the back of my hair, sending tingles down my spine while her lips sent my heart through my chest. It wasn't a passionate kiss that we shared, but one of longing. I felt as though I'd wanted her my entire life. As if I'd been searching for her all this time and had only now remembered. Her breath escaped as I kissed her, as if she was as surprised as I was by the pull of it. Her fingers brushed against my throat and moved beneath my ear as she kissed me.

And then, at the height of our perfect moment, she tensed and pulled her lips from mine. Her fingers moved repeatedly just below my jaw, leaving me breathless.

"Where is your scar?" Her voice no longer held teasing as she continued to press her fingers against the place in question.

Reality doused me like cold water. I exhaled slowly, defeated, as her fingers moved to my hand once more, as if she was inspecting me through a different lens.

Her breath caught as she began to put the pieces together. She stepped out of my embrace and turned from me to flee. I couldn't simply let her leave after a moment like that.

I reached out and took her hand before she was out of reach.

"Please, don't leave. I can explain." I didn't even care how desperate my words sounded. She let out a small gasp at hearing my voice, further confirming her suspicions.

"What have you done with him?" she asked, all sweetness gone. "Did my uncle put you up to this?" She stepped backward while I still held her hand.

"I assure you, miss, no one has put me up to this," I said quickly.

"Why did you not make your presence known when I first appeared?" she asked curtly.

"I was rallying the courage to, but . . . "

She slipped her hand out of mine and rushed for the door.

"Please, may I have your name, miss?" She was moving too fast. She was going to slip away—"Please!"

She opened the door a sliver, then just as quickly rushed out.

I stood there, glued to the spot, like an idiot, for what seemed a lifetime before I rushed after her.

But by the time I threw the door open and looked down the corridor, it was empty.

She was gone.

CHAPTER 2

Wooden paneled walls and old paintings passed in a blur as I rushed down the hallway. I couldn't let her slip through my fingers so easily. I had to find her. Before I knew it, the ballroom and its many guests materialized as I stepped through the threshold of two large doors. The exhale that escaped my lungs next was one of frustration, for I was greeted by a sight that made my task seem impossible. Women . . . everywhere.

Dread plummeted into my stomach as I looked at them all. How was I to find *her* in all of this? What did she look like? Was she beautiful? Plain? Dark or light haired? What color were her eyes?

Scanning the room, I weaved a path through the outskirts. Would she appear flustered from our meeting? I grasped for any information I knew about her that could help me.

Her hands! They were bare when they touched mine.

Taking courage, I walked the entirety of the outer floor, eyes jumping from woman to woman, examining each hand. To my dismay, every woman in the room had gloved hands. Lady Mystery had either left the party or had put her gloves back on. Deep-brown eyes with matching deep-brown hair suddenly met mine for a moment before they looked away quickly. Was she the one I was looking for? I had no reason to believe that she was, other than the fact that she was a woman. My eyes continued combing the surrounding area, and I was soon met by another woman's green eyes, accompanied by a kind smile. Another set of brown eyes with honey-colored hair, blue eyes with auburn hair. My heart pounded faster and faster.

Someone bumped into me as I searched without direction. I opened my mouth to utter the words, "I beg your pardon," to find that I had run into a woman. She was beautiful, with honey-brown hair and light-hazel eyes to match. Was this my mystery woman?

"I beg your pardon," she breathed as she curtsied, then turned and moved on. But she wore gloves just like the rest. She was a lady, just like the rest.

I inhaled deeply to calm the escalating taunt of one thought:

You will never find her.

I suddenly wished I had paid more attention to Mrs. Hale's prattlings earlier that evening. Had she mentioned a lady who lived with her uncle?

Mrs. Hale.

If someone could help me solve this, it was she. I spotted her grey hair and inquisitive look almost immediately. I parted the guests and moved in her direction. When she spotted me, however, her brow raised with displeasure, her mouth pressing into a firm line. Then she turned away from me. I raked a frustrated hand through my haphazard hair.

That's what you get for walking away in the middle of her sentence, you idiot.

I let out an exasperated breath at my own stupidity. Mrs. Hale would not help me now. A few more ladies' eyes met mine as I scanned the room once more. Any one of them could be my mystery lady. I couldn't exactly walk up to each of them, wrap my arms around their waists, close my eyes, and kiss them one at a time, discovering which one felt just right.

That kiss . . .

How long would she have let me kiss her if . . . I shook my head before I finished the thought. I couldn't help but feel conflicted about the entire thing. I felt guilty for letting her believe I was someone else. Then again, I had tried to speak out multiple times. And I wouldn't take back the experience for anything. Something had come alive in me at that moment, and I didn't regret how it had played out.

I only regretted that I had not done more to discover her name before she ran off. I would do anything to find her now. A stab of guilt suddenly plagued my conscience.

I was being selfish. She would be better off if I left her alone. She was already in love with someone else.

I rubbed my fingers over my chin, at war with myself.

She may be in danger, I argued with myself. She said her uncle may kill her before he sends her away. I nodded my head. Yes, I had to at least find out who she was to ensure her safety.

Just as the thought occurred to me, I sucked in a quick breath, realizing what it would mean. If I was to find Lady Mystery, I would need to do something I hadn't undertaken in years. My time for being an unsociable creature was over. Necessity demanded that I not only speak to ladies this evening, but dance with them as well.

Where to start?

I hadn't the first clue how to solve this type of mystery. I wasn't so concerned about whether she was the most beautiful lady in the room or the most plain. I cared only that I found the right one. It wasn't surprising that in my mind I could imagine her both plain and striking. Either way, I wanted to be near her more than any person in existence. I decided I would start somewhere between absolutely beautiful and plain. I looked at the room and made a mental list of which ladies I would ask to be introduced to first.

Now for introductions. I scanned the room. I'd blown my chance to have Mrs. Hale's assistance. Then my eyes settled on my closest friend, Stephen Bentley. He was the most eligible gentleman in all of Bath, and he knew everyone.

FIVE DANCES in and I felt only slightly closer to finding Lady Mystery. None of the women so far seemed to match *her* exactly. But I wasn't able to distinguish anything absolutely. When Miss Wycliff spoke, I was positive that her voice didn't match. But then she spoke with a smile, and I wasn't completely certain anymore.

I concluded that her hands weren't a match and that she couldn't be Lady

Mystery. Then again, did her hands feel different simply because she wore gloves now? I couldn't exactly pull them off and find out. I had the genius idea to ask if she hated her uncle, but what kind of question is that? Labeling myself as an odd fellow wouldn't help my case to impress her.

Unfortunately I found a different dilemma when I danced with Miss Pembroke, someone I was relatively acquainted with. I thought of a clever way to ask about uncles.

"Miss Pembroke," I said, trying to form a smile but only managing one that felt awkward. "I have recently discovered that I am an uncle. Do you have any uncles?"

She gave me a questioning look before she said, "Mr. Livingston, I was under the impression that you hadn't any brothers or sisters."

Nice going, you idiot.

I held my awkward smile in place as I thought of a way to look slightly less ridiculous. My burning face graciously reminded me that my cheeks were a shameful color of red.

My eyes caught Stephen, surrounded by a myriad of ladies. He had many nieces and nephews, the lucky devil. He had just told me earlier that evening that he was a new uncle for the 13th time. An idea sparked in my mind.

I laughed, hoping to dispel some of the awkwardness from our lingering moment of silence. "Indeed you are correct, Miss Pembroke. I have no brothers or sisters. But Mr. Bentley is like a brother to me. And if he is once again an uncle, then so am I."

Part of me inwardly rolled my eyes at my own stretch of the truth. True, Stephen would have shared anything with me. But I wasn't exactly at liberty to claim his family as mine. Fortunately, it did the trick on Miss Pembroke. Her eyes softened and she gave me a sweet, pretty smile.

"That is so very sweet of Mr. Bentley." She glanced over at Stephen with dewy eyes. At least it told me one thing—she wasn't Lady Mystery—for Miss Pembroke clearly had eyes for Stephen. And last I checked, Stephen did not have a scar below his ear that followed his jaw line.

The other three gave nothing substantial to prove they were my mystery lady.

Miss Crawford laughed too much. Miss Seymour was bored to death. Miss

Salisbury was accomplished, or so she said, but she adored her uncle. Not one of them felt right.

I was now beginning my sixth dance of the evening. My feet were screaming at me for standing up for each dance set when I was not usually accustomed to doing so. I was currently dancing with a woman named Miss Ivy Fortescue. She was beautiful, with large, wide-set eyes the color of a stormy sea and thick blond hair that curled near her face. She had a lovely smile, and perhaps her voice even matched my mystery lady's, though it was hard to tell in a room so full of noise.

When I asked if she had any uncles, I took courage when she responded with, "Indeed I do, Mr. Livingston, but I'd rather not talk about my uncle just now."

I tried to act normal as I realized I had most likely been kissing this woman in the dark mere hours ago. I did have to admit that dancing with her in the light wasn't as exhilarating as holding her in the dark. Regardless, I was intrigued. And she really was one of the most beautiful women in the room.

"Miss Fortescue, do you enjoy reading?" I asked. It was one of the only things I could think of to ask.

Her eyes lit up. "Indeed, sir."

I smiled with satisfaction, knowing we had at least one thing in common. By the time our dance concluded we had discussed a number of topics. Politics, poetry, composers, and operas. We were very alike, and we shared many of the same views. She had to be my mystery lady. Once again, I reflected on the fact that it didn't feel the same dancing with her as it had when she was secured in my embrace, our lips meeting. But that made sense. All in all, I was thrilled to have finally put the pieces together. And I loved knowing what was inside her head.

When the dance came to a close, I walked Miss Fortescue back to her party. A cross-looking woman greeted us, her aunt no doubt.

I searched my brain for something clever to say before I left Miss Fortescue, but Stephen's voice sounded by my side before I had the chance.

"There you are, old chap." Stephen grinned in his foppish way. "I wanted to introduce you to a few more ladies, since you have chosen tonight to come out of hiding." Stephen dipped his head toward the beautiful lady I had just relinquished from my arm. "Miss Fortescue."

She dipped a curtsy. "Mr. Bentley." Her eyes quickly found the floor.

Stephen looked back at me. "Mr. Fortescue does not like to be kept waiting." My friend gave me a knowing look and cocked his head toward a severe-looking gentleman standing a few paces off, fixing me with a firm stare.

Mr. Fortescue? Did her uncle share her same last name? Or was Stephen referring to her father?

It was silent for a moment, and I realized it was my turn to speak. I looked back at the stormy-eyed woman. "Thank you, Miss Fortescue, for standing up with me." I managed a genuine smile.

She returned it with a pretty smile of her own then answered with, "The pleasure was all mine, Mr. Livingston."

When Stephen had led me away some paces, I stopped him.

"Is that severe-looking man Miss Fortescue's uncle?" I blurted out.

Stephen cocked an eyebrow and grinned as if he found something particularly amusing. "I have heard of your recent obsession with uncles since you just became one yourself to my new niece." He paused for dramatic effect, then smirked. "Congratulations."

I rolled my eyes, but my face grew hot with embarrassment.

"I didn't realize you wanted to be an uncle," Stephen said with mock pity as he pulled out his elegant pocket watch, breathed warm air on its face, and rubbed it against his overdone blue-and-yellow striped vest. "You could have been an uncle 13 times over if you'd only told me your heart's desire." He finally looked at me, this time with a serious expression. "Why the sudden interest in being uncle to my niece?"

Stephen usually played the part of fop and dandy. But I knew better than to push him when he wanted an answer. He would get his answer one way or another.

I looked down at the floor. "I just needed to ask Miss Pembroke if she had any uncles. But it felt odd asking her outright. So I told her I had just discovered that I was a new uncle before asking if she had any uncles. It was quite awkward, however, when she called my bluff, reminding me that I have no brother or sister, and I said the first thing that came to my head." I knew I was rambling. But I wanted it over with.

Stephen stared at me without a grin or smirk. It was an expression that was impossible to read.

"It won't happen again," I said awkwardly.

Stephen studied me for a moment longer before he finally asked, "And pray, tell. Why, exactly, are we investigating Miss Pembroke's and Miss Fortescue's uncles?"

"Nothing worth mentioning, really." I tried to sound calm, but my heart was beginning to speed up.

Stephen knew my one weakness. He folded his arms then continued to stare at me, not breaking eye contact for a second.

I looked away, but it was no use. I could still feel his eyes on me. Fleeing was an option, but I knew from experience that Stephen would just follow me around until I finally broke. I tried folding my arms, staring back at him to see if it was my lucky day and he would finally break first. It was no use. He had been beating me at this game ever since we were boys.

I finally relented. "I'm trying to figure out which of these ladies has an uncle who is potentially threatening her and sending her away in three days—and I don't know her name."

Stephen's hard stare finally subsided and his eyebrows creased in confusion. "Point her out and I'll tell you her name."

How much more humiliating could this get?

I looked away, annoyed. "I don't know what she looks like."

Stephen's mouth parted into a smile, and he laughed, leaving his foppish demeanor behind. "You may be unyielding at fisticuffs and holding your ground against a man, old chap." He slapped my back. "But you are completely incompetent at wooing a lady. Let me guess: You retired to the blackest, coldest room you could find, as usual, only to overhear gossip between two ladies. And now you must solve the mystery . . . and maybe even assert yourself as a protector for the lady in distress?" He raised his eyebrows. "Has a mysterious lady finally caught your eye?" He chuckled at his words, then said, "I guess she didn't catch your *eye*, since you live in the dark. Has she captured your heart before you even know what she looks like?

I shook my head, pretending to be irritated, but grinning just enough that he would think he was right. In truth, this was the perfect cover for what had really happened. And now Stephen could possibly help me. I wasn't getting anywhere dancing with ladies at random and hoping to find out if they hated their terrible uncle. It reminded me why Stephen and I were having this conversation in the first place.

"Now." I folded my arms. "Is that severe-looking man Miss Fortescue's uncle?"

Stephen breathed in slowly, then nodded his head. It was an odd reaction, as if he wasn't telling me the whole of it.

CHAPTER 3

I looked over at Miss Fortescue in the distance, then back at my friend. A sinking feeling settled in my gut. Did Stephen pine for Miss Fortescue? My eyes quickly flew to Stephen's ear, then traveled to where my mystery lady had felt with her fingers when discovering that I did not possess a scar. I found nothing. I gripped Stephen's arm and quickly jerked him around so I could inspect his other side.

Nothing. I breathed out in relief.

"What the devil?" Stephen muttered before he gripped my arm and murmured, "There is something you aren't telling me. Courtyard, now." He gave me his unyielding stare once more and nodded to the doors leading out to the terrace, waiting for me to move outside. I felt less frantic knowing Miss Fortescue was my mystery lady and relieved that Stephen did not bear the scar she had searched for. But there was something I was missing.

When we reached the courtyard, Stephen wasted no time.

"What are you leaving out?" he demanded.

"I'll tell you when you tell me," I retorted, this time feeling confident enough to give him a stare of my own as I folded my arms.

For the first time since . . . well, ever, he relented first. He threw his hands up in the air then blurted out, "I never anticipated us both pining after the same woman."

A knot formed in my stomach. If it was a lineup between Stephen and me, he would win every time. He would probably even win against Mystery Lady's scarred man if he tried.

"I see," I said, trying to sound unaffected. "Then I wish you both happiness."

"That's just it. She hasn't eyes for me. I've tried to win a laugh from her on more than one occasion with no success. A smile from her would send my heart racing. But she seems completely unmoved by my antics."

I thought on this for a moment before I decided to give him one more piece of information.

"She is in love with someone else."

"How would you know that?" Stephen asked, narrowing his eyes.

I finally thought of a way to enlighten him without divulging the truth entirely. "I didn't overhear two ladies gossiping in a room about a sinister uncle—" I paused. "It was a lady and a gentleman, with whom she is most definitely in love. She told him that her uncle will send her away in three days if he doesn't kill her first. I was able to see their outlines, but they weren't able to see me. She traced her fingers just below his ear and down his jaw line and asked him if his scar still hurts." Hopefully Stephen wouldn't see that this part of my story was a downright lie.

His eyes sparked with understanding as to the reason I'd been examining his jaw. "And here I thought you were trying to dance with me." His mouth twisted up on one side, but I sensed it was done only to humor me. Something still ate at Stephen.

He exhaled in defeat. "And yet, I saw you pull not only one, but three smiles from Miss Fortescue this evening. Something I have only dreamt of doing. Are you sure you are not the man who holds her heart? And if you're not that man, how did you get her to smile? And don't lie to me. I'll be able to tell."

Thankfully, I could be completely honest about this. I nodded. "I promise I am not the man who holds her affection. Before tonight I didn't even know of Miss Fortescue's existence." The truth of it hit me forcibly. If I had made an attempt to get to know her before this scarred man had claimed her heart, would she love me instead of him? It was enough to make me go mad, realizing I had been wasting my time as a lone man, fading into the background at balls and parties. If I couldn't have Miss Fortescue, then perhaps I would try again with someone else, though it was already impossible imagining any other woman fitting so perfectly in my arms or kissing me so completely.

"And how did you get her to smile?" Stephen prodded.

I folded my arms across my chest and finally said, "I asked her questions."

"*I* ask her questions," Stephen said almost defensively.

"I didn't act like a fop," I said, raising an eyebrow.

Stephen was silent for a long while as he let my words sink in.

Eventually his voice filled the silence as he extended his hand out to mine. "May the best man win?" he grinned, a spark of hope taking shape in his eyes. "If you truly have been unaware of her existence until this evening, then surely it cannot be so great a loss for you if I do finally win her heart. I've been trying for months now, but if her heart does turn to you in the end, I will not take it upon myself to hate you for all time." He finished his last words dramatically, then gave me his typical wink.

"What a relief." I smirked back. But how could I explain to him that the brief moment I'd shared with Miss Fortescue wasn't simply a moment that couples experience while dancing, or talking, or flirting, or even courting? It was a moment when her soul had opened to mine. Nothing felt more right than it had in that moment. But I was only one half of that equation. Miss Fortescue had opened her soul to me thinking I was another man. A man that she already loved and trusted. I couldn't let this consume me. I nodded to Stephen and gripped his hand. "And I promise not to hate *you* for all time when she chooses you over me."

We shook our hands before Stephen added, "Now let's go find this scarred man and ensure that Miss Fortescue is not in danger. Though Miss Fortescue's uncle isn't one that I would suspect as a murderer, he is certainly severe. We must make doubly sure she is safe."

This we both agreed on, and without another word we strode side by side back into the ballroom.

CHAPTER 4

We had a plan to draw Mr. Scar, as Stephen now called him, out. Stephen had a habit of drawing attention to himself at large parties. Whether it was due to his ridiculous foppish way of speaking and telling stories or the fact that he was the most eligible bachelor in Bath I could not say. But ladies and gentlemen alike would crowd around him as he would dramatize the simplest of tales, true or false, and eventually the gentlemen would join in the fun and the ladies would fawn over him. It was absurd, and it was the reason that Stephen and I usually only ever interacted outside of social settings.

Today, however, we had an act to perform and Miss Fortescue's scarred man to draw out.

Stephen stood in a spot full of ladies and gentlemen. I shook my head as he overtly squared his shoulders and puffed out his chest as if he were the most important man imaginable. He then made passing comments to each man and woman, both polite and ridiculous. The thing that surprised me the most was that he knew each of them by name and seemed to know a detail or two about each person's life. The ladies gave him demure smiles, and the gentlemen gave him jovial nods.

When a large enough crowd had formed around him, I stood next to him and said loudly, "If I'm not mistaken, Mr. Bentley, you have neglected to tell this lovely group the rapturous story of the time you brandished the stick sword, obtaining your nearly lethal battle scar."

Stephen quirked his lips in a foppish way, then said, "Hear, hear, old chap. It is a wonderful story indeed." His story was then related with every inch of theatrical finesse I would expect.

Another gentleman I was unacquainted with added his bit once Stephen had concluded his story. "I once acquired a scar from tip to tail on my finger from carving a stick." He backed it up by showing the crowd his index finger, then added, "I thought the blood would never stop. I nearly fainted for all the blood I lost."

"Oh heavens," one of the ladies said next to him as she blanched.

"There is a sizable scar on my leg from tripping over our groundskeeper's ax!" another man blurted out.

They were taking the bait. I gave Stephen a knowing grin, then folded my arms and enjoyed the scene as, one by one, men gathered and women stepped out of the ranks. Did the men all stand a little taller as they related their heroic stories?

I turned my head every which way to see the newcomers—and then I saw him standing two gentlemen away from me. A quiet observer with brown hair, styled fashionably, and blue eyes, standing amidst the other gentlemen—with a scar starting just below his ear, then trailing beneath his jaw toward his chin. He smiled genuinely as he listened to each story.

"And what about you, sir?" I nodded in his direction. "What is the story of your glorious battle scar?"

He humored me with a small grin before he said, "I'd rather keep some stories to myself."

Blast it all, he was taller than me.

And handsome.

I smiled in a friendly manner to the gentleman, then set my jaw when he looked away. Apparently it wasn't enough to have Stephen as competition.

He's probably dull, lacking a sense of humor, I thought, attempting to console myself.

But then the thought occurred, *I do believe you are describing yourself.*

My mouth formed into a rigid line as I acknowledged the truth. "Mr. Scar" was actually Lord Perfect. And he held Lady Mystery's heart for good reason. He wasn't only taller than me, fashionable, and handsome, but he also appeared to be humble enough to deny the spotlight just now. Adding to that, he wore an affable smile and had a good-natured look about him—something I lacked.

Blast it all, Lord Perfect.

Surely I should give up this ludicrous venture. Besides, what would I ever say to convince Miss Fortescue to choose me over this man and Stephen?

"Excuse me, Miss Fortescue, but we shared a kiss in the dark moments ago, and I do believe it would be wise for you to leave the man who holds your heart, in addition to the most sought-after bachelor in Bath, in order to make way for me. All I ask in return is that you will you speak often, and be near me, preferably close enough to be held and kissed—many times."

I shuddered just thinking about the uncouth monstrosities that could spew from my mouth if I did actually confess all. Yes, I had better leave it be.

But the thought alone felt like a betrayal. Her kiss lingered with me even now, an all-consuming reminder that the moment we'd shared would haunt me forever if I didn't at least try to win her heart. Stephen hadn't heard of any engagement between Miss Fortescue and a gentleman. Therefore, she had not yet been spoken for. If she chose Stephen in the end, or *Lord Perfect*—I would give her up and be happy that she was happy.

Stephen's eyes eventually found the mystery man with the scar. Understanding dawning in his eyes, he looked at me, and I nodded before stepping out of the cluster of gentlemen. It was almost time for the next dance set to commence. I stood a ways off from the group and watched as Stephen finally bowed out of the group and joined me. We observed this mystery man for a moment as he continued to watch the group relate their stories with a genuine smile.

"I don't much like the look of him," Stephen said, a grin on his face.

"Do you feel threatened, Mr. Bentley?" I asked in mock pity.

"Dear fellow, that will never do," Stephen said, putting on a dramatic look of melancholy. "Of course I feel threatened. He may not be as striking as I am," he said with ridiculous pomp, "but he certainly is handsome, and that will not do if she is already in love with him. I might as well be invisible."

He had a point. And now Mr.—I wasn't sure what to call him—was leaving the group and heading toward us, no doubt to claim Miss Fortescue for the next dance. Stephen and I looked at one another briefly, and he smiled as if he'd won a small fortune.

"You've already danced with Miss Fortescue tonight. So unless you plan on proposing this evening, I believe it's my turn." Stephen turned and walked briskly in Lady Mystery's direction.

Thus it begins. I exhaled.

I looked over at Miss Fortescue and realized there were a number of eligible ladies in her party. Five, to be exact. If I could dance with one of them, perhaps I could obtain more information about Miss Fortescue's uncle and decide if she truly was in danger. My eyes settled on two ladies whom I had noticed earlier that night.

Stephen was already approaching their small group. He dipped his head properly and addressed Miss Fortescue and her uncle. As before, she looked at the floor as soon as it was deemed proper and averted her eyes away from him.

Odd. She'd seemed at ease with me. It gave me a small sliver of hope as I approached the party as well. Three of the four ladies were smiling, holding back giggles as they watched Stephen talk to Miss Fortescue and her uncle. The fourth lady, with dark, honey-colored eyes and hair was observing the ballroom. Our eyes met briefly before she looked away.

I came to stand next to Stephen. I had already been introduced to Miss Fortescue and her uncle by Stephen, but now I needed an introduction to these other ladies—especially if they were going to help me discover the truth about Mr. Fortescue. I nodded to each of them as they looked at me. Only three of them smiled back genuinely; the women with honey-colored eyes gave me only a cursory look before continuing to scan the ballroom.

It took Mr. Fortescue a moment to recognize his duty to perform the introductions. He set his jaw in what appeared to be annoyance with the task at hand, then finally said, "Mr. Livingston, Mr. Bentley, these are my nieces, Miss Ivy Fortescue, Miss Eleanor, Miss Katherine, and Miss Anne." He then pointed to the lady with honey eyes and huffed as he said, "And this is my ward, Miss Eliza Wood."

They all curtsied in our direction as we dipped our heads.

Stephen smiled. "Miss Fortescue." He looked at her with eyes that spoke of admiration and gave her a sincere smile that he usually didn't let out at social events. "Would you do me the honor of the next dance?"

I was already regretting the advice I gave Stephen earlier. Miss Fortescue looked up at him, a look of surprise filling her features momentarily before she covered the expression.

"It would be my pleasure," she said, seeming somewhat perplexed, before she took the arm he extended towards her.

Anger would not help my mission now. I looked to Mr. Fortescue. "Sir, may I dance with your ward, Miss Wood?" I figured that Miss Fortescue's sisters might not answer me truthfully if they were in danger. But a ward might have a more objective opinion.

He shrugged in annoyance and was about to turn around but stopped cold in his tracks, narrowing his eyes and staring just beyond me. In a cold, angry voice, he said, "She's already dancing with someone else." I turned to leave but found Mr.—Scar? Lord Perfect? *Him*—behind me. I realized that Mr. Fortescue had been talking to him, not me.

The scarred gentleman looked over at Stephen and the eldest Miss Fortescue lining up to dance, then responded to her uncle. "I wondered if Miss Eleanor would do me the honor," he said.

The lady in question smiled and stood, waiting for her uncle's permission. "Oh, please, may I dance, uncle?" I looked over at Miss Eleanor and took in her deep-brown eyes and hair to match. Her voice sounded like Lady Mystery's as well. Especially when she smiled as she spoke. I looked over at Miss Fortescue. Did I have the wrong lady?

Her uncle barked at the man standing behind me. "I'm no fool," he said with cold calculation before he turned to me. "Well, why are you still standing here? Are you going to dance with Miss Wood or not?"

This man was getting on my nerves.

"I do intend to dance with Miss Wood," I said matter of factly. "I do not intend, however, to be spoken to as if I were your servant, Mr. Fortescue." I took a step toward him, and his eyes bulged in surprise as I lowered my voice and spoke curtly. "I suggest you watch your mouth, sir, before it gets you into trouble."

I looked over at Miss Wood and felt a pang of guilt as she looked at her guardian with embarrassment at the spectacle he was making. I wasn't helping matters.

"Is that a threat?" Mr. Fortescue bellowed.

I offered the lady my arm before I turned back to Mr. Fortescue.

"Believe me, sir," I said in a clipped tone. "If I was threatening you, you would know it."

CHAPTER 5

M iss Wood grasped my arm more tightly than most ladies would have felt proper as I accompanied her to the dance floor. Perhaps I had put her in a situation that would make life harder when she returned to her guardian's home. I studied her expression as she stood across from me. She really was beautiful. Her honey eyes were discerning and observant. Without a single exchange of words, I could tell she was keeping an eye on Miss Fortescue, Stephen, Miss Eleanor, Mr. Mystery, and Mr. Fortescue. When her eyes finally found mine, she jumped slightly, as if she was not expecting me to be watching her. When the music began and our hands came together, I asked my first question, though it wasn't the question I had originally planned.

"Miss Wood, are you well?" In truth, she looked as though she was trying to bury her nerves.

She looked up at me and did her best to smile. I could tell it was meant to appease me. "Do I not look well, Mr. Livingston?"

Her voice was mostly strong, and I could almost believe that she truly was well. But her voice was overcompensating, betraying subtle hints of anxiousness.

"You look very well, Miss Wood. I am only concerned that my exchange with your guardian has distressed you."

"He always distresses me," she said flatly. Our hands fell apart, and we circled away from each other. She was trying so hard to keep her voice steady. I wondered if she was putting up barriers to keep from falling apart.

When she came to stand in front of me once more, the dance steps required that I bring one hand up to her waist while the other took her hand in mine. I noticed dried tear streaks on her cheeks. They only appeared at one angle, when she was facing the majority of the candles. I had the oddest sensation to brush the streaks away, despite the fact that they were already dry. I felt for her plight. She had little control over her situation; she was at the mercy of a man with a hot temper and bad manners. I looked over at Miss Fortescue, then to Miss Eleanor. They all were at his mercy. I glanced at Miss Eleanor and—Lord Perfect.

I really needed to call him something else.

"Miss Wood, who is that gentleman dancing with Miss Eleanor?" I moved my eyes over to the man in question.

She watched him for a time with a blank expression before she finally answered. "That is Mr. Davis." There was a melancholy to the way she said his name.

"And why does he bring sorrow to your eyes?"

She looked at me with surprise, as if she hadn't been aware her feelings were so apparent.

I didn't know how to speak with women. Therefore, it didn't surprise me that I was most likely overstepping my bounds. I didn't expect her to answer something so personal. But she surprised me with a long exhale before she spoke.

"Mr. Davis was betrothed to Miss Fortescue. My guardian broke off their engagement three summers ago due to family reasons, and he refuses to let Mr. Davis anywhere near the house. He was like family before Mr. Fortescue cut ties. Life isn't the same without him."

"And does Miss Fortescue still find ways to see him?"

She looked toward Mr. Davis and Miss Eleanor dancing, then said, "I guess we all see him in our own ways."

I looked out at the dancing couple as well and tried to put the puzzle pieces together. Was Mr. Fortescue opposed to Mr. Davis being with any of his nieces? How did Miss Fortescue feel about it? Were they still secretly meeting? Hoping to get married?

My eyes returned to Miss Eliza Wood's. This time, I was startled to find that she was watching me. A small wave of electricity rolled over my stomach, causing my pulse to quicken as she studied my eyes. I tried to remind myself to say something and to try to at least appear normal.

Her eyebrows creased, most likely at my inability to form words, before she asked, "Are *you* well, sir?"

I couldn't help but chuckle at the question she turned back to me. "Do I not look well, Miss Wood?" I smiled.

She gave me a small grin. "Are you in need of flattery, sir, or would you like it straight?"

She was teasing me. It was as I watched her lips that I finally realized something. Her voice, too, sounded like Lady Mystery's. Did everyone in the Fortescue household sound like *her*?

I needed to hear her speak with a smile. I grinned, then did something I had never done in my entire life. I thought of Stephen and his ridiculous charade, and said in the most foppish way I could muster, "Come now, my lady. A man is always in need of flattery. And I am no exception."

A small laugh escaped her lips before she did her best to bite it back, along with her smile.

Gratified that I had succeeded in shocking a smile out of her, I notched an eyebrow. Now I only needed her to speak with a smile in tow. "Now, Miss Wood." I dropped the foppish charade, but used an easy, affable tone. "I do believe that only the sweetest words of flattery will suffice. They may be untrue as long as I believe them." I gave her a challenging grin, curious whether she would humor me.

She looked at me, deciding. I could see the debate she was having with herself before her grin faded. "I'm sorry to disappoint you, Mr. Livingston. But I won't say something unless it is true."

I did my best to swallow my disappointment. "I understand," I nodded. "There is nothing flattering you can say that is true." I still smiled, but her implication stung.

Her eyes found mine immediately, and she looked surprised at my words. "No sir, you misunderstand me." She moved her hand up from mine and gripped my arm briefly to emphasize her point.

I froze as she did so, my pulse racing. She felt so much like Lady Mystery.

At that moment, the dance steps required us to step apart once more. I found myself frozen, looking for her as she moved behind another man and weaved in and out of a few more people dancing. I had no more answers. Miss Fortescue sounded like Lady Mystery and was beautiful and enchanting. And she hated her uncle. Miss Wood sounded exactly like Lady Mystery and had grabbed my arm in the exact same way. But Mr. Fortescue was not her uncle, and Mr. Davis had been wishing to dance with Miss Fortescue, not Miss Wood.

I searched the sea of moving men and women but couldn't find my dance partner. What was taking her so long to come back to me? And then I finally saw her making her way back through the steps. When she came to stand in front of me once more, instead of barely placing my hand about her waist, and letting her rest her hand in mine, I pulled her in closer than before.

Her breath caught and she looked at me, speechless.

"How did I misunderstand?" I asked, wanting to hear her speak again.

She swallowed visibly before she finally responded. "Because I don't know you, Mr. Livingston. And if I say flattering things to you, they will be true. And if they are true, then it could only be because you mean something to me."

Her eyes had me completely entranced. On top of it, I had to will myself *not* to glance at her lips. Her words had pierced me, and her voice pulled me. I knew her story didn't line up with Lady Mystery's, but Miss Wood felt more like *her* than even Miss Fortescue had. Eliza Wood's soul spoke to mine in a way I couldn't put into words. I looked at her hands, wishing I could take them in mine, without gloves.

I remembered what I needed to ask Miss Wood, but not before I said one more thing. It took some control for me not to stroke her cheek to see if her skin was just as soft as my mystery lady's. Instead I moved through the steps, applauding myself for keeping her where she was rather than pulling her even closer. "Miss Wood." My eyes returned to hers. "I love your sincerity. I know we are barely acquainted, but your soul feels honest and kind. I hope you'll not change."

She looked at me for a moment as if she was trying to solve a puzzle before she averted her eyes once more. Miss Fortescue may have been a more striking beauty than Miss Wood, but Eliza's eyes were captivating. They conveyed so many unspoken words.

"I hope we can be friends," I said, reminding myself not to pull her closer to test my theory that she felt like Lady Mystery. "Friends are allowed to mean something to each other."

She looked at me again with that puzzled look before she lowered her voice. "Forgive me for seeming strange, Mr. Livingston. But have we met before?" She studied my eyes as my heart pounded at her attention. She looked down at our hands as they came together before she looked at me once more. "It's just that you seem so familiar to me, but I can't place why that would be." Her eyebrows creased as if a thought suddenly entered her mind that hadn't been there before. She appeared to dismiss it almost as quickly as it came.

What would she do if we had indeed shared that kiss and she then discovered it was me? I could ask her outright if she had found herself away from the ballroom at any point. But I suddenly cared a bit less about finding Lady Mystery's true identity and cared more about staying in Miss Wood's good graces. I concluded once and for all that Miss Wood was not my mystery lady. All evidence pointed to Miss Fortescue.

"Perhaps I seem familiar because we are meant to be friends," I finally said with a matter of fact tone.

"Perhaps," she said, somewhat guarded.

Now to finally ask my question. "Miss Wood. I wanted to ask if your guardian, Mr. Fortescue, is a danger to you or any of his nieces. Forgive my assumption, but he doesn't exactly seem the loving type."

A grin played on her lips at my last comment. "What would have given you that impression, sir? It wouldn't happen to be the way he speaks to anyone and everyone, would it?"

I chuckled. "Certainly not, miss. I have no idea to what you are referring."

A soft smile tugged at the corners of her lips, making my heart pick up speed. I wondered what a full smile would do. But she had dodged my question, and I was in earnest.

"Miss Wood, you have still not answered my question. Are you in danger?"

She exhaled then dropped her eyes to the floor. "I hardly know, sir. I always feel as if he is on the edge of harming me or one of his nieces. He has only ever hit me when his rage gets the better of him, and it isn't as often as one might think. I am not naive, however, and I know this kind of treatment is not so uncommon. It could be worse, and I've never needed to be seen by a doctor after one of his storms."

I tensed as she related this information. I suddenly felt the desire to whisk Miss Wood and the Fortescue sisters out of the ballroom and hide them away in a safe place where they could no longer be hurt by this tyrant. I needed to find a way to protect them. Surely Stephen would help too. And possibly even Mr. Davis.

My eyes met Eliza's just before the dance steps, once again, pulled us apart. I told myself to keep her at the same distance when she came back to me. But try as I may, my arm wound a little tighter around her waist, protectively, while my other arm took her gloved hand once more.

She took in a quick breath when I brought her closer and averted her eyes just past my shoulder, as if she hadn't expected to be brought so near me. But she didn't pull away, so I didn't loosen my hold on her.

We passed a small moment in silence before I finally asked, "Have you no other place to go?"

Her eyes hesitantly returned to mine before she slowly shook her head. "No, sir. I have no other place to go unless I wish to go to the workhouse."

An icy chill went up my spine as I imagined her in such a place.

"And his nieces?" I asked. "Do they have anywhere else to go?"

She nodded. "They are leaving Bath in four days to return home with their papa. He has been overseas, but he has since returned home to Lancashire."

"And they will leave you?" My eyebrows creased in concern. "Can they not take you with them?"

Miss Wood blinked several times as if she were forcing tears back. "They are technically no relation of mine, though they are like dear sisters to me. They come and stay with Mr. Fortescue for a time each season, and then they return home."

Tears collected in the corners of her eyes until a tear leaked out on each side. She quickly dried them with her gloved fingers. Her dried tears from earlier suddenly made more sense. This woman was to be alone with her malicious guardian in four days, without the company of her dear friends.

I wanted time to stop so I could ask her more questions. I wanted to watch her soulful, dark-honey eyes and the unspoken words they told. But I knew our dance would soon come to a close.

"Miss Wood, may I call on you tomorrow?" I asked. I would come whether she said I could or not, simply to make sure the Fortescues and she were safe.

Her eyes were laced with pleasure at my suggestion but overshadowed by doubt. "You may try, Mr. Livingston. But I would be astonished if Mr. Fortescue actually permitted you to step foot into the house. Mr. Davis has tried many times, as well as other suitors, but all attempts these last couple years have been in vain."

I raised an eyebrow. "Perhaps these suitors lack something that I possess."

"And what is that?" One side of her lips turned up.

"A backbone."

CHAPTER 6

Stephen and I leaned against a marble pillar, where guests were sparse, as we discussed what we had discovered.

"Mr. Fortescue is indeed sending his nieces away in four days," I confirmed. "And Miss Wood is to live with the ruffian without the company of other ladies."

"Indeed." Stephen muttered. "And Mr. Scar—"

"His name is Mr. Davis," I interrupted.

Stephen looked over at me and raised his eyebrows. "I do believe I like Mr. Scar better. It has a certain ring to it. But if you insist, Detective Edward, then Mr. Davis it is."

I rolled my eyes at the childhood name. "What have you discovered?"

"I have discovered that Miss Fortescue is the most splendid woman of my acquaintance. Did you know she has committed to memory every single one of Lord Byron's poems from hours of idleness?"

"Absolutely thrilling," I said dryly. I certainly wasn't jealous. "And did you do anything useful this evening in regard to ensuring her safety?"

"I didn't realize you were in charge, Detective Edward."

I shook my head. Again with that name. "As it happens, I did discover that she met with Mr. Davis this evening."

"She confided in you this information?" I asked, offended that she would trust him so easily.

"Don't sound so surprised, old chap," he chuckled. "And she may have been somewhat coerced." He gave me a sheepish look. "I told her I have been keeping an eye on her uncle for a few months now, since he has been found withholding funds due to important men."

"That's false, and you know it," I retorted.

Stephen gave me a flat stare. "Would you like the information or not?"

I folded my arms and nodded for him to proceed.

"I told her I have been tasked to keep an eye on all of them to ensure their safety." When I scoffed he said, "It isn't a lie. You have asked me to do just that. Now stop interrupting me or I'll keep the rest to myself."

Sometimes I really just wanted to punch Stephen's stupidly perfect face. But I held my tongue and allowed him to proceed.

"I told Miss Fortescue that I had followed her out of the ballroom to make sure she wasn't being lured or blackmailed, and I told her that I saw her enter a room and later, after watching that same room I saw a man enter the room as well. I pointed out Mr. Scar—excuse me, Mr. Davis—as that man, and she became a bit flustered, stating that it wasn't what I thought.

"I told her I was thinking only of her safety and that her secret was safe with me. She said they were discussing what to do about Miss Wood. The Fortescues are worried for her safety when they leave in four days, and Miss Fortescue is hoping that Mr. Davis can help Miss Wood once they leave, though he is not allowed near the house. They worry that she will waste away or be hurt. She asked me to befriend Miss Wood and make sure she is taken care of."

She *hadn't* told Stephen about our kiss in the dark. I was relieved. But was Miss Fortescue lying about her meeting with Mr. Davis? Or had she met him later after our shared kiss?

Stephen looked solemn for a time. "I feel for Miss Wood. She will be completely alone in four days with no company other than a tyrannical guardian and his stiff, unfeeling wife. I assured Miss Fortescue that I would visit her friend every day that I am able to break away."

If I had been jealous about Stephen's success with Miss Fortescue, it was nothing compared to what I felt at picturing Stephen sitting alone with Eliza

Wood and her dark, honey eyes, bringing smiles to her lips or embracing her as she cried.

I didn't exactly mean to shove Stephen in my irritation. But I did.

"What the devil was that for?" he said, actually annoyed.

I pushed aside my regret at giving Stephen pointers earlier, then said, "Did you know Miss Fortescue was engaged to Mr. Davis?"

Let him chew on that, I smirked.

"Engaged?" His eyebrows creased. "As in past tense?"

"Indeed. Her uncle broke off the engagement, but it appears as though she still pines for him. And based on the fact that they met alone in a dark room, and that he came to ask her to dance moments after you did, proves that he still loves her too."

"Blast it all," Stephen grumbled.

I couldn't help but grin at his look of jealousy. I understood him perfectly. And in that moment I realized something. I didn't want to compete with Stephen. Even more than that, as exhilarating as sharing a perfect kiss with Miss Fortescue had been, I felt more for Eliza. I cherished that one moment in the dark with Miss Fortescue more than I actually enjoyed her company face to face. But Eliza—she was someone I wanted to be with in the light.

I looked over at Stephen. "I have decided to forfeit my plans to win Miss Fortescue's heart. You have had your eyes set on her far longer than I have."

Stephen looked at me long and hard with a straight expression. "Why the sudden change of heart?"

I debated how much I should confide before finally responding, "I believe Miss Wood and I are better suited," was all I offered as a response.

"Well then!" He slapped his hands together in excitement. "I can pursue Miss Fortescue without feeling conflicted, and I will help you secure Miss Wood."

I held back a grin as my plans began to shift. "I believe we should call on them tomorrow." I paused as I found Mr. Davis across the room smiling and laughing with the Fortescue sisters and Miss Wood. "And I believe we will need Mr. Davis's help."

Stephen's smile fell back into a straight line before he folded his arms and moved his eyes to where Mr. Davis stood. He looked over at me, clearly unconvinced and blandly said, "If you say so, Detective Edward."

CHAPTER 7

The plan was simple. Stephen would call on the Fortescues while Mr. Davis and I watched from a short distance. Stephen would be congenial and affable. If he was admitted entrance, we would follow him inside. If he was turned away, I would try a different tactic . . . with a little more force. If that didn't work, we would sneak inside—which is why we needed Mr. Davis. He knew the layout of the house.

I was surprised at how easy it was to convince Mr. Davis to help us. To Stephen's chagrin, Mr. Davis was kind, easygoing, and willing to do anything to help the Fortescue sisters and Miss Wood. If he was concerned that two other gentlemen were calling on Miss Fortescue or any other of the ladies in that household, he hid it well.

Stephen paced in front of the Fortescues' door, posed dramatically, and then shook his head and paced again. Then he stood rigidly, head held high, chest puffed out, and raised a fist to the door. But just as he was about to knock, he shook his head again and repeated the process.

"What is he doing?" Mr. Davis asked.

I grinned. "Mr. Bentley believes a first impression is paramount to impressing one's company."

"And is he intending to impress the ladies? Mr. Fortescue? Or the butler?" He chuckled.

Stephen finally knocked on the door and settled on a natural pose with his hands behind his back.

"Mr. Bentley, Mr. Davis, and Mr. Livingston to see you," the butler announced.

By some stroke of luck, Mr. Fortescue and his wife were not home, and the three of us were shown into the drawing room without any resistance. The doors opened to the Fortescue sisters, Miss Wood, and an elderly woman acting as chaperone. My eyes immediately found Eliza as the women stood and curtsied.

The women looked at one another with wide eyes and shocked expressions, apparently as surprised to see us in the drawing room as we were to have been shown inside so easily.

"Please do have a seat," Miss Fortescue smiled, looking at each of us. "Tea will be brought in shortly."

As we took our seats, I felt the need to pull at my cravat for the sudden heat that sprung to my neck and cheeks. Being in such close quarters with so many pretty women at once was not something I was accustomed to. I may have felt bold the night before, and I would have had no problem being forceful with my speech to Mr. Fortescue had the occasion necessitated it. But now, sitting across from five young ladies, I found myself holding my breath, with a mind completely blank, mouth dry, completely a coward.

Thankfully Stephen took over, and I was able to breathe again.

"I trust you are all well since we saw you last night?" Stephen smiled with ease.

"Indeed," Miss Fortescue smiled back softly. "And I trust you are all well?" She looked at each of us. I managed a nod, then looked at the floor.

"I am very well now that I am here with my favorite people in all the world," Mr. Davis said with a genuine smile. How were these men able to be at ease in a situation like this?

Stephen gave Mr. Davis a tight smile, as if the man had beaten him to the punch. "Indeed," he said as his eyes turned to Miss Fortescue. "I have dreamt of little else but seeing your faces again." His words included all of the women, but his eyes stated that he spoke only of Miss Fortescue.

I held back a smirk as I watched my friend try to outdo Mr. Davis. I finally dared another glance at Eliza. But she, too, was watching the exchange between Stephen and Mr. Davis.

Her eyes fixed on Mr. Davis. "And are you acquainted with these gentlemen? Or did you simply happen to call on us at the same time?" She looked once more to Stephen and then to me. Her eyes lingered on mine for a moment before she looked at Mr. Davis once more.

"These gentlemen are not only acquaintances, but friends," he said sincerely. "They wish to help each of you. I would call anyone with such an objective my friend."

No wonder Miss Fortescue was drawn to him. He embodied goodness. Stephen must have been thinking the same thing, for he looked over at me and gave a forced smile. No doubt his conscience was beginning to plague him, realizing he was trying to come between Miss Fortescue and this good man.

"How do you plan to help us?" Eliza asked, turning her eyes to mine.

If only her eyes didn't put me in some sort of trance. If only there had been a class at Eton on how to speak to beautiful women who do strange things to your heartbeat.

"I, er—well that is—we would like to—" I looked over at Mr. Davis and Stephen for help. Stephen was holding back a laugh, but Mr. Davis held an affable smile, as if it was the most normal thing in the world to hear me stumble over the most basic words.

"You would like to what?" Eliza prompted, pulling my eyes back to hers.

The thought of our dance and her hand in mine suddenly gave me the confidence I needed. "Between the three of us, we intend to check on each of you every day to ensure Mr. Fortescue is not treating you ill," I said, surprising myself with the confidence I heard in my voice.

"Are you in earnest?" Miss Katherine asked, a hand to her heart. "I've never heard of a kinder gesture."

"Nor I," Miss Anne and Miss Eleanor said at the same time.

"And how do you plan to get past the gargoyles?" Eliza smirked as she looked between the three of us. "They are not usually away. And they don't let anyone past the front door."

"I'm glad you've asked," I grinned back at her, taking courage. "Would you be willing to meet us somewhere specific each day at an allotted time?" I glanced at the older lady. "Chaperoned, of course." I nodded to her and she acknowledged it with a bow of her head.

"We could meet at the edge of the garden, behind the stone wall." Eliza's eyes lit up as she said it. "One o'clock in the afternoon. They never go to the gardens unless absolutely necessary."

"Wonderful!" Mr. Davis said, smiling at Eliza. "It is settled then."

"In that case," I said, standing and addressing Eliza. "I believe we must be going before said gargoyles return." Mr. Davis and Stephen stood with me, followed by each lady present. They curtsied, and we dipped our heads in their direction. But before we left, Mr. Davis took each of their hands in his and bowed over them in farewell. Stephen watched, and then, when Mr. Davis had concluded his farewell, Stephen took Miss Fortescue's hand and pressed a light kiss to it. Her breath caught, and she blushed.

"Please meet me tomorrow," he said quietly to her, not caring to hide his affection. It was a bold move, and I felt for Mr. Davis. Miss Fortescue said nothing but continued to look at Stephen until her eyes eventually broke from his and she found her sisters' eyes, Miss Wood's, and Mr. Davis's. Her blush deepened as she realized everyone had witnessed Stephen's open affection for her. She suddenly walked out of the room, the back of her hand held to her cheek.

For once, Stephen looked unsure of his actions. I glanced at Eliza, and she smiled back at me, raising her eyebrows. Did she approve of such behavior between Stephen and her friend?

"Well then." I raised my eyebrows at the awkward silence now filling the space. "Until tomorrow."

Stephen walked out briskly, followed by Mr. Davis. I slowly moved to the door, then stopped when I heard footsteps behind me. I turned to find Miss Wood behind me. She fidgeted with her hands, then walked up to me.

"Thank you for calling on us today," she said, taking another step toward me, holding my gaze.

"I told you I would." My words came out quiet. I had the desire to reach out and touch her hand. She was so lovely.

"I should have believed you," she smiled. She took one more small step towards me, then quickly turned my hand over until it opened. I found myself entranced by this simple move. She deftly slipped a small piece of parchment inside my palm and closed my fingers around it. I finally understood that she was trying to slip me a message unnoticed. Her back covered our hands from view, so her friends could not see the exchange. I quickly put my hand in my pocket, then took in her eyes once more before I nodded in her direction and exited the room.

CHAPTER 8

F our hours later, I fidgeted just outside the Fortescue garden waiting for Miss Wood. I read the message over and over as I waited at the meeting place. The message contained only five words.

Meet me tonight at dusk.

I hadn't told Mr. Davis or Stephen about the note. It felt personal, and my heart pounded at the very thought of meeting her out here when the sky cast cool tones across the earth. I watched in the direction of the house, waiting for any sign of movement.

"You came!" her excited voice chimed behind me.

I clutched my chest, startled, my breath coming rapidly from her sudden appearance.

She bit her bottom lip as if she'd been caught doing something naughty, then chuckled at my surprised expression. I looked around for her chaperone. She was nowhere to be discovered.

I opened my mouth to say something, but she had rendered me speechless. I couldn't stop thinking about why she would bring me here. Did she feel something for me, as I did for her?

"I'm sorry if I startled you." She grinned. "I have learned to move quietly. It's better if my presence goes unnoticed."

Her implication tore me up inside, and I found that I wanted to render Mr. Fortescue unconscious. I couldn't fathom how she must be feeling, living with an abusive tyrant, knowing her only friends and companions would be leaving her in only a few short days.

She stepped closer, setting my heart racing. She then lowered her voice so her next words barely came out above a whisper. "Thank you for meeting me here, Mr. Livingston. I have a thought, and I wanted to get your opinion."

My opinion? My excitement dropped slightly at the realization. *No confessions tonight,* I frowned inwardly. But I recovered quickly, happy to be in her presence regardless of the reason.

"And what thought do you have?" I asked.

She smiled with enthusiasm. I couldn't help but look at her lips when she did it. I found her eyes once more as she began to speak.

"I believe your friend Mr. Bentley has formed an attachment to my dear friend Ivy."

"What ever gave you that impression?" I teased.

She swatted my arm playfully. "Don't laugh at me. Ivy is more dear to me than any friend in the world. I would love to see her happily settled, and I believe she has had feelings for Mr. Bentley for some time now. Today only confirmed my suspicions, and I wanted to see if you would help me."

She held my gaze, unsure of how I would respond. I wanted to please her, but I had a lot to consider. I wasn't so convinced that Miss Fortescue did actually have feelings for my friend. How could she when she had just kissed Mr. Davis—well, *me*, with such sincerity and had held to him—me—so lovingly? Was Stephen a good match for Miss Fortescue when she already loved Mr. Davis? Then again, I didn't really know Mr. Davis, and I *did* know Stephen. He would treat her with love, kindness, and respect.

I decided it wouldn't hurt to go along with it and let Miss Fortescue choose in the end.

"What do I get in return?" I lifted a corner of my mouth in jest but prodded to see her response.

"I haven't anything to give you, sir." Her eyes dimmed as if she believed I wouldn't help her because she had nothing to offer.

"I don't want money, Miss Wood, if that's what you think." I looked at her. "I'm sure we can put our heads together and think of something. How are you at swiping goodies from the kitchen?" I teased.

"I hardly ever risk such a venture, sir, in fear of Mr. Fortescue discovering me."

I wanted to slap myself for not considering such a thing.

"What else do you want?" she asked, folding her arms.

Looking at her in the cool tones of dusk, I knew exactly what I wanted. I wanted this woman to let me discover exactly who she was. I wanted her to look at me with excitement, and I wanted to know it was because of *me*. But I couldn't exactly tell her that.

"How about you tell me your plans, and then I can tell you what I want in return for my assistance?"

She smirked. "Very well. I have only three days before Ivy leaves for Lancashire. What if we create small ways for them to meet until she leaves and see what comes of it?" She beamed with enthusiasm. I couldn't help but smile.

"Three days of matchmaking," I grinned, "in exchange for three requests."

"What kinds of requests?" she asked.

"I won't know until we arrive at that moment. But you are free to decline my requests until we settle on something with which we are both satisfied."

A breathtaking smile parted her lips. "So you will help me?"

"I will help you," I echoed, smiling in return.

"Then you will receive four requests," she grinned. "You may have one tonight as well for meeting me and for agreeing to this plan."

I liked the sound of that. And I already had an idea of what I wanted, though it would seem odd.

"Very well. Let's begin our plans." I motioned my hand to a stone bench and waited for her to sit. I took a seat next to her, and then we planned.

Eliza smiled as we concluded our secret project. It was nearly dark, and I needed to return home. I stood from the cold bench and immediately missed the warmth Eliza had brought.

"I must be going," I said quietly. "I worry you'll be discovered if you don't return to the house."

She nodded, then stood as well. "And what request would you like from me tonight?" she asked.

I breathed in and debated whether or not I had the nerve to ask.

"Your hands," I finally said.

"You want my hands?" She smiled. "I'm sorry, sir, but I'm afraid they won't come off."

"No, I don't want your hands—" I shook my head, somewhat embarrassed before I finally blurted out, "May I examine them?"

"You want to examine my hands?" She still held a smile, but confusion was etched in her voice.

I had been thinking of little else since her fingers had slipped the note into my hand. Her hands were elegant and graceful, and I wanted to hold them in mine and feel them to see if they felt similar to Miss Fortescue's when she had put her hands to mine in the dark, or if they were completely different.

She was looking at me now with a curious expression. "Why do you want to examine my hands?" she asked.

"We didn't agree upon an explanation for my requests. Only that you may accept or decline them." I took a step closer to her. "So what will it be?" Her eyes glistened in the low lights of evening, turning into night. "Do you accept or not?"

She looked nervous, as if she didn't know how to respond. Then, just as I became convinced she would refuse me, she let out an exasperated sigh and said, "Very well, you may examine my hands." Uncertainty laced her voice, but she drew her hands up towards mine and allowed me to hold them.

They were freezing, like Miss Fortescue's had been that first evening. They were slender and smooth like hers, too. But Eliza's were even more perfect because they belonged to her. I slowly turned her palm upward, then gently coaxed her fingers open. I looked at her fingers as I traced each of them with mine. Despite her freezing hands, warmth spread through me at the touch. She held perfectly still, hardly breathing. My eyes finally met hers in the darkness.

"Your hands are freezing," I whispered.

She only nodded as I lifted them towards my face. I carefully opened her fingers once more and held them against my cheek. I repeated the process with her other hand and held my hands against hers for a time until the iciness from her fingers left their mark upon my skin. Then I gently moved them back down my cheek, grazing my lips on their way down. She watched me, speechless, before she finally cleared her throat and took a step back from me, breaking our connection.

"Goodnight," she whispered. "Don't forget our plans for tomorrow."

A longing settled in my chest as she moved away from me.

"Goodnight," I uttered as she turned. I had some secret plans of my own, and they all included Eliza Wood.

CHAPTER 9

The plan was supposed to be simple. Stephen, Mr. Davis, and I had originally intended to take one day each for the next three days to meet at Mr. Fortescue's house at the allotted time and place to ensure the safety of each lady residing there. But now, Stephen insisted that he must come along on my turn in order to see Miss Fortescue. And Mr. Davis stated that he would be most grateful to come along as well. I, for one, could not get Eliza out of my mind and wanted as many occasions as possible to see her.

After a short debate, it was decided that we would all go together on each meeting.

We didn't wait for more than a minute or two before Miss Fortescue approached the bench, looking back toward the house every few steps. We fought over a small hole in the wall that allowed its viewer a perfect window into the Fortescues' back garden.

I finally had a good view when Stephen moved me to the side.

"You can't have all the fun," he said, peering through.

A feminine giggle echoed behind us, making us jump. "I didn't dare come through the back garden for fear that Uncle Fortescue would see me."

Stephen quickly straightened and smoothed his vest and waistcoat. Was that a look of embarrassment on his face? If so, it was gone as quickly as it came.

"Miss Fortescue," he said, lifting his top hat and dipping his head in her direction. His eyes were only for her.

I refrained from shaking my head at Stephen's boldness . . . barely.

"How do you all fare?" Mr. Davis finally asked, claiming Miss Fortescue's attention.

"Yes," Stephen said, inserting himself. "Has your uncle yet been horrid enough for me to whisk you away from this prison?"

She grinned but shook her head at his antics. "How outlandish you are, Mr. Bentley."

"Then I won't be whisking you away?" Stephen asked with a shameless grin.

Her cheeks turned a pretty shade of pink as she bit back a smile. "No, sir."

I glanced up at the dark, imposing roof of Mr. Fortescue's house, still visible from where I stood. I was just able to make out a top window above the fence. My heart skipped as I recognized the eyes peering out.

Eliza.

She raised her hand and waved it in greeting. Warmth spread through me, making me feel more alive. I smiled and began to mirror her action. As I lifted my hand to wave, a movement did the same in my periphery. I looked over to find Mr. Davis waving as well, eyes averted to the window. When I returned my gaze to Eliza's, I realized she wasn't looking at me, but him. I hated the flare of jealousy that inserted itself inside me. I quickly doused its flames. Of course she would seek him out first. He was a lifelong friend. And I could see how much he cared for each of these ladies.

Her eyes finally found mine and a mischievous smirk formed on her lips as if we shared a secret. I dipped my head and returned a smile.

Indeed, there was no need for jealousy. *I* was the one with whom she shared her secret plans.

Two hours later I returned to the exact same place, Stephen in tow. The plan

Eliza and I had made together was clear: I was to bring Stephen to the meeting place at 3 o'clock for their first "chance meeting."

"Now, remember to stand watch the entire time," I said to Stephen as seriously as I could manage. We once again had come to the hole in the stone wall. "I am determined to examine the house and find a way to break in, as a precautionary measure, of course. You must whistle our secret code as loud as you can if I am to be discovered."

He cocked an eyebrow. "I don't think so. *I'll* go map out an escape route, and *you* can stand guard."

"You only want to see Miss Fortescue," I said with a smirk. "I will actually get the job done."

Stephen put on his foppish stance, then said, "Right you are, Detective Edward. I will wait here and give you five minutes."

I shook my head. "I'll need at least ten."

"Very well, make it quick." He dropped his ridiculous voice and sat on the stone bench that jutted out from the stone wall, then added, "You owe me." He peered through the hole and observed the house as well as he could.

I smiled as I disappeared around the house and out of Stephen's view. Once out of sight, I strode to the copse of trees where Eliza would meet me.

If all went according to plan, Eliza would bring Miss Fortescue around the house from the front, claiming they needed a long walk. Halfway to the meeting place, where Stephen waited, Eliza would tell her friend that she had left her shawl inside and that she must fetch it. She would then tell Miss Fortescue to wait for her on the bench.

Eliza would meet me here, where we would watch Ivy and Stephen without being seen.

Five minutes later, Eliza neared our meeting place. She wrapped her thinly covered arms around herself, no coat or shawl, clearly freezing. Her nose and cheeks were nipped from the chill air, while a breeze danced around her hair, which was partly up. The rest of her hair flurried softly around her shoulders.

I wanted nothing more than to wrap her up until she was warmly secured in my embrace.

Eliza's eyes found mine, and she smiled.

My heart skidded about. She was breathtaking with her eyes alive with excitement. It was hard to think about watching Stephen and Miss Fortescue when all I wanted to watch was her.

She entered our little sanctuary and let out an excited breath as she came to stand in front of me. "You've done well, Mr. Livingston. Everything is going according to plan."

"I didn't realize our plan included you catching your death. I insist you wear my coat." I looked at the thin fabric lining her arms and raised an eyebrow in censure while I started shrugging out of the warmth of my coat.

"I refuse to wear your coat, sir," she said stubbornly, taking a step away from me. "If I take it, *you* will certainly catch *your* death, and this was all my idea to begin with." She folded her arms. "And you may scold me for not wearing something warmer, but I couldn't wear a coat or shawl; otherwise Ivy would have never believed my story." She lifted an eyebrow of her own as if her explanation should have been obvious.

I took my coat off despite her refusal and held it open for her, trying my best to make it look as enticing as possible. "Please, miss, I really do insist."

"And I insist that I will not take it. Will you also insist on wasting our time when we should be observing our friends?"

I exhaled in frustration. "Is there nothing I can say to persuade you?" I shook my head at her stubbornness.

"I daresay there is nothing you can do to change my mind."

She looked colder by the minute. "Then at least go back inside and retrieve your coat."

She put her hands on her hips and pursed her lips, as if she knew exactly what I was up to. "If you don't want to wait here with me and you are trying to send me away so you can sneak off, you are more than welcome to do it while I'm present."

Part of me wanted to smile at her adorable expression, while the other part of me was hurt that she had such little faith in me.

"Miss Wood." I took a step towards her and placed both of my hands on either side of her shoulders. "I wouldn't leave you."

Her eyes softened as she studied mine. I was convinced I could be content to peer into her eyes forever. She slowly nodded and said under her breath, "Yes, I believe you wouldn't. But I don't dare waste any more time retrieving something warmer. I'll be alright."

My pulse came alive from her nearness and searching gaze. Her chilled rosy cheeks and windswept hair were absolute perfection. She looked away from me. Something resembling regret entered her eyes before she shifted to the side, making my hands fall away from her shoulders. She walked to a place where she could easily observe Stephen and Miss Fortescue, then turned her head back toward me.

"And now we watch." She grinned, but it was laced with hesitance.

I stepped up next to her. "Isn't this all a bit untoward?" I teased.

If I had been a man who cared about society's rules, I would have found her behavior alarming and improper. But as I couldn't care less about society and its many rules, I found it charming.

"Oh, hush." She nudged my arm playfully. "I'm trying to watch, and you're ruining it." She glanced over at me. "And believe me, sir. When you live with Mr. Fortescue, the last thing you want to be called in public is untoward. But in this case, they aren't alone. We are chaperoning them."

"Then who is chaperoning us?" I chuckled.

She turned to me and put her hands on her hips and pursed her lips, considering. She finally looked up at the branches and said with flat mockery, "The birds."

"There are no birds in this tree," I said just as dryly, giving her my best impression of a serious school master.

She continued to hold her look of feigned stubbornness. When she looked at me that way—lips pursed, eyebrow cocked, hands on hips—I found it impossible to keep my pulse in check.

Her nearness made it nearly impossible to keep from looking at her lips. I looked over her shoulder instead.

Eliza must have thought she'd won this little battle of ours, for she smiled triumphantly, then turned back toward Ivy and Stephen. A quiet giggle escaped her mouth as she watched Miss Fortescue look down from Stephen's gaze.

"She's blushing." Eliza smiled.

We watched our friends for a time until Eliza eventually turned toward me and gave a grateful smile.

"Thank you for helping me today, Mr. Livingston. And I'm sorry our winged chaperones weren't doing their job properly."

I faced her and tried to bite back a grin. "I'm discovering that I appreciate their bad manners," I said quietly while leaning in just barely. She held perfectly still, not daring to meet my eyes. It was hard to understand Eliza Wood. Each time our eyes met, I felt that she both wanted and rejected my attention toward her. Was this how all ladies worked?

I inwardly shook my head, then took out my pocket watch. I exhaled regretfully. We had been away for as long as I dared risk. I wanted to stay, but I didn't want Eliza or Miss Fortescue to suffer the wrath of Mr. Fortescue if they were discovered.

"I must be going soon," I said begrudgingly. "And as such, I believe it is time for me to claim my second request.

She pressed her lips together, as if she was nervous to discover what my second request would bring. Trying to mask her expression, she said with a teasing tone, "Now that you have examined my hands, as per your first request, would you like to examine my feet as well?"

I couldn't help but chuckle. "Would you *like* me to examine your feet?"

She opened her mouth, apparently shocked that I would suggest such a thing, and her cheeks turned a lovely shade of red as she began to shiver from the cold. I really needed to find a way to get her warm.

"Absolutely not!" She tried to hide an embarrassed smile as she swatted at my shoulder.

I caught her fingers before they made contact and watched her reaction. She appeared to be at war with herself. Leaning into my touch, but also watching our fingers as if she shouldn't want them together.

Her eyes met mine, that conflicted look returning to her gaze as she slowly pulled her fingers away. We stood so close together.

"What is your second request?" she asked, barely above a whisper, now watching my hands as if transfixed by them.

I tried not to feel too discouraged by her response. "Not your feet, Miss Wood, but your arms."

"My arms?" she laughed quietly. "What ever do you want my arms for?"

"Mostly, I just want to get them warm. You're shivering." I nodded to the thin sleeves enveloping her.

"And how do you suggest we do that?" She tilted her head and raised her eyebrows at me, waiting for my response. "You already know I'll not take your coat."

"I will show you, Miss Wood. And if at any point you object, I will choose something else."

"Very well, I've been warned." The corner of her mouth turned up.

I unbuttoned my coat, then slowly took her icy hands in mine. She watched me as I carefully placed her hands inside my coat and around my waist, allowing the fabric of my coat to envelop her arms completely. Her breath came out faster, but she didn't pull away. I finished by pulling as much of the fabric of my coat around her as I could and wrapping my arms around her back. She tensed slightly and studied my eyes.

I leaned in near her ear. "Is this alright?" I whispered, hoping I hadn't overstepped my bounds.

She stayed perfectly still and rigid for a moment before she slowly relaxed. I let out a quiet breath of relief and inched her closer to me little by little, feeling the coldness of her hands penetrate through my clothes. My heart thudded through my chest as she slightly moved her hands up my back and laid her head on my shoulder. I closed my eyes and drank in the moment.

"Is it working?" I breathed next to her ear. "Are you warm?"

"Yes," she whispered, melting into me further.

The warmth I felt in that moment wasn't the kind I could measure in degrees. It was a warmth that started in my heart, beating in rhythm with hers, then spread to every single inch of my body.

I wanted it to last forever. But as most good things come to an end, I had to eventually let her go. Before I did, I brushed my fingers through her hair once and whispered, "I'll be here again tomorrow afternoon, as we planned."

She nodded, then looked at me for only a split second before she slowly removed her hands from around my back and leaned away from me. I immediately missed the feeling of her in my arms.

As she pulled away, I reached out and took her hand in mine once more. "Please go directly inside once you've claimed Miss Fortescue. It really is much too cold."

She nodded once more before I released her. She immediately wrapped her arms around herself, already beginning to shiver, and walked away.

CHAPTER 10

Today's plan was essentially the same as yesterday's. This time, however, Miss Wood would bring a blanket and a small basket with buttery bread and strawberry preserves for Ivy to take the rest of the way.

"A woman is even more irresistible when she provides an equally irresistible dish," she had said to me when we first concocted these clandestine meetings.

I was already waiting for Eliza in our little copse of trees. Stephen hadn't cared what excuse I gave him today. He gladly accepted the task to "stand guard."

Though I knew I shouldn't hope, part of me wanted Eliza to come without her coat again today. I had relished the feeling of her so close to me, and the memory of it had kept me awake for hours that night. I hoped she felt about it as I did. Something ate at Eliza, and it was keeping her from letting me in fully. I could only pray that today I would have more success.

Minutes later I watched through a slit between the trees as she walked swiftly toward our meeting place, a knitted shawl about her arms. Though it would keep her warmer than the day before, it was thin and worn, and I loathed her guardian even more in that moment. Why did Mr. Fortescue not buy her a proper coat, or a thicker shawl at the very least? It was a well-known fact that he wasn't wanting for money.

She looked apprehensive as she approached. I wanted to ease whatever worry was on her mind. I wanted to bring that breathtaking smile to her lips.

She hadn't noticed me yet, and I suddenly had the idiotic notion to hide. I concealed myself in the perfect spot, between a bush and one of the trees. I heard her footfalls enter the space, and she sighed. It sounded as if she was relieved. My heart faltered, and I suddenly felt ridiculous for hiding. I peered out from behind the bush and paused at what I saw. Her face showed sheer disappointment. I bit back a smile, gratified that she did at least want my company.

"Where are you, Mr. Livingston?" she muttered so quietly that I wondered if she'd said it at all.

She turned her back to where I hid and looked to where I'd left Stephen. I quietly crept toward her until I was standing just behind her back. Her head tilted in confusion, most likely because she had spotted Stephen and was wondering where I was.

"Are you looking for someone?" I asked in a nonchalant tone, as if I was asking about the weather.

She gasped and whipped herself around. When she realized how close I was standing to her, she took a quick step backward, losing her balance. Before she tipped over, I steadied her. I may have put an arm around her back in order to do so.

Her eyes focused on mine, and she opened her mouth slightly, as if she wanted to say something to scold me.

"Have you been here all this time?" she finally asked, sounding appalled.

A grin tugged at the corner of my mouth. "I believe that depends on whether or not you wished me to be here all this time." I hoped she wasn't truly angry. But she hadn't yet pulled away from me.

She glared at me, though there wasn't much power behind it.

"Miss Wood," I finally said, intending to change the subject. "I hardly think this is warm enough." I used my other hand to brush her shoulder where the thin shawl rested. "Is this the warmest thing you own?"

Her jaw tensed as if she was embarrassed by my question, then pulled away from me and uttered the words, "It is, sir." She held her head high and stared at me boldly, as if she wouldn't be bullied by my disapproval of her attire. It tore at my heart. Did she think I judged her for it?

"I believe your guardian and I may share a few words after today," I muttered under my breath. "And possibly fists as well."

She looked at me with surprise until her eyes softened. And then I saw it in her eyes. Admiration. She wanted to let me in. Warmth spread through my chest as her eyes slowly opened a small window into her soul, ready to show me everything. Then, as if she sensed it too, she quickly looked away, as if she had woken just in time to close her ears from the siren's call. The warmth fled, and I was left with only longing.

She tried to give me a smile, but it was forced. "We had better chaperone our project," she said, walking to the place where we'd watched Stephen and Miss Fortescue the day before. Did she have any idea how much she made my heart race? Did she have even an inkling of how much my heart ached when she pulled away from me as she had just done? I exhaled slowly, then found my way next to her.

She attempted another smile. "Do you not think they balance one another perfectly?" Our eyes met once more, and I could see how much she wanted to show me what was hidden. But just as quickly as the thought came, she looked back out to our friends.

I didn't care about whether Stephen and Miss Fortescue were well suited. All I cared about at that moment was discovering why Eliza wouldn't let me in.

And then I knew what my third request would be.

CHAPTER 11

I humored Eliza for a time and watched Stephen and Miss Fortescue. And she was right, they were a good match. I could see that Stephen was genuinely smitten, and Miss Fortescue seemed equally enamored with my friend. They didn't seem to notice time or our absence as they talked and smiled at one another.

After a few minutes of watching them, I turned my face toward Eliza. "I believe it's time for my next request."

Her face was close to mine, and when she dared to meet my eyes, she swallowed visibly before looking away.

"What is your request?" she asked, holding her breath.

I was silent for a moment before I said, "Your soul." I was hoping my answer would shock her out of this unreachable state.

It did the trick. She reared her head back in shock and scoffed. "My soul? What are you, a witch?"

"I'm a warlock, actually," I said dryly, lifting a corner of my mouth.

She breathed out a laugh, "Well I'm sorry, Mr. Warlock Livingston, but you can't have my soul, because it's mine."

"And what makes you think I want to steal it?"

"Well, what else could you possibly want with it?" She gave me a challenging look.

"I only wish to examine it," I said nonchalantly.

She looked at me with an unreadable expression. "And how, exactly, Mr. Warlock Livingston, would you examine my soul?"

I took a steadying breath, hoping I wasn't ruining my chance with her by being so bold. "They say the eyes are a window into the soul. And I would like to know exactly which shade of honey yours are."

She breathed in slowly, debating. "I can tell you what color my eyes are, sir." She refused to meet my gaze. She was beginning to shiver again, as if the very idea of my request made her feel vulnerable.

"Are you denying my request?" I asked. "I can think of something else if this makes you uncomfortable."

"And what would you request next?" She tried to keep her tone light, but there was accusation beneath the surface. "My heart?"

I didn't answer for a moment. I looked back out at our friends before I finally said, "I can see that I have overstepped. Please forgive me, Miss Wood."

She looked up at me, appearing conflicted by my response.

"What if we try something less vital than your heart and soul," I suggested with a lighthearted grin. "What if I request that you wear my coat so you don't catch cold? If you die tonight from this cold, then we will never be able to finish our meddling. And we both know that Mr. Bentley and Miss Fortescue would never fall in love without our meddling."

"Then you would be without a coat, sir, and you would catch *your* death."

"Are you stating that you would prefer my earlier request?" I smirked.

She cocked an eyebrow, clearly not amused, then let out a relenting sigh and said, "Very well, I will wear your coat."

I smiled, then shrugged out of it, holding it open for her. She turned her back towards me and put her arms inside, then gathered it around herself. She slowly shifted around until she faced me once more. She looked absolutely adorable with my sleeves hanging past her hands and the fabric around the shoulders swallowing her up.

She wrapped her arms around herself and breathed in with satisfaction. "I don't know why I argued with you. This warmth is divine. I'm afraid I may not give it back."

A chill already began seeping through my sleeves, and I chastised myself for not finding a way to make her take it sooner. She must have been freezing.

"Then you may keep it for now." I gestured to my coat. "Besides, it looks far better on you than it ever looked on me."

She rolled her eyes but wasn't quite able to bite back her smile.

I resumed my position of observing our friends. She followed my lead and stood close at my side. Her warmth was both a joy and a curse, reminding me that she might never want what I wanted.

We passed a considerable amount of time in silence, waiting in the comfort of one another's unspoken thoughts. Eventually, Eliza's melodic voice pierced the quiet space between us.

"Mr. Livingston. Do you truly believe that you can look at one's eyes and see the soul?" She sounded genuinely curious.

A corner of my mouth turned up, and I looked over at her. "I do."

She gave me a challenging look, as if she didn't believe me, then looked back to Ivy and Stephen. "And why do you believe that looking at someone's eyes can show you their very core?"

I turned myself to face her as she continued to look out. I took one more small step towards her until her shoulder brushed against my chest.

"*Looking* alone tells nothing," I said, studying her delicate profile and dark lashes. "But searching . . . " I slowly lifted my hand toward her face. If she opposed in the slightest, I would leave it be. But if she—

My fingers gently brushed beneath her jaw and slowly turned her face toward mine. Her breath caught at my touch, but she didn't shy away.

Her eyes found mine—and slowly that small window began to open once more. Her lips were close, and I wanted to feel them against mine more than anything. But for this moment, I simply drank in her honey eyes. My heart beat wildly as I felt her goodness and sincerity, her longing, her heartache. Passion and fear. She was letting me in. She wanted—

Her eyes closed suddenly, and she let out a shaky breath. But she didn't move away from my touch that still held her face close to mine.

I trailed the back of my other hand softly against her cheek. "What don't you want me to see?" I whispered.

Moisture collected at the corners of her closed lashes.

"So many things," she finally whispered, a tear rolling out of the corner of her eye.

"What things?" I asked as I continued to slowly brush my fingers against her skin.

Her hands raised to where I touched her face, her fingers taking hold of mine and hesitantly lowering them, as if she welcomed my touch but shouldn't. She looked at me with a tortured expression.

"I am terrified," she breathed. Another tear ran down her cheek. "My uncle plans to send me away to who knows where once the Fortescues travel home to Lancashire. He detests me more than anyone. No one knows of his plans except for me. Not even Ivy knows. I overheard him speaking to my aunt a few nights ago, and I haven't the heart to tell the others. They will only worry incessantly without the ability to help me." Her hands began shaking, and a quiet sob escaped her lungs.

I felt as though my entire world was plummeting to an endless pit of impossibilities. She *couldn't* be sent away. I couldn't help but wrap her in my arms as she cried. She needed comfort—and she felt so wonderful leaning against me. She fit so perfectly right where she—

The realization hit me like a tidal wave. I had held Eliza Wood in this exact way before. I had already tasted her perfect lips and felt her soul—

I closed my eyes in dread and breathed in slowly. "Miss Wood?" I finally asked, my words coming out barely above a whisper. I didn't want to ask my next question, but the words came out regardless. "Did you say Mr. Fortescue is your uncle?"

She nodded and let out another shaky breath.

Dread filled every inch of me as the missing pieces slowly fell into place. My voice sounded hollow as I said my next words. "Why does your uncle introduce you as his ward?" It was the only thing I could think of to say. I still held her close, realizing that this would be the last time I would be able to do so.

She took some time to answer my question. "My uncle despises me, just as he loathed my mother. It's complicated. My mother was Mrs. Fortescue's sister. From the moment I arrived on my uncle's doorstep, he has insisted that I never call him uncle, or talk about our relation to one another in public."

I exhaled in anguish and put to memory exactly how she felt against me. Her light floral scent as her hair shifted, and her heartbeat against mine. Her words confirmed my suspicions. Not only was she Mr. Fortescue's niece, but she was Miss Eliza Mystery Wood . . . and she was in love with someone else.

She held tight to my embrace for a time until her tears stopped. The ache had already settled in when she slowly pulled away from me, as if her conscience demanded it.

"Mr. Livingston, there is something else you should know." She looked at me once more with that tortured expression before she said, "I am in love with—"

"Mr. Davis," I finished. My eyes found hers, and inside them I found confirmation.

"Yes," she whispered.

Despite the fact that I had already discovered the truth, my heart plummeted at hearing her confirm it.

She took in a slow breath, then let it out. "George and Ivy were intended for one another before either of them could crawl. Their parents had arranged their union. But they never felt for each other in that sort of way, though Ivy and all her sisters love him dearly—as he loves them.

"When George started visiting us during the summer seven years ago, he and I formed a close friendship and bond. Friendship turned to something deeper, and by the time I was 17 we were secretly engaged. Ivy and her sisters were more than happy for us and gave their full support. Ivy too had fancies of marrying for love and was grateful to cut their betrothal.

"But when Mr. Fortescue discovered our attachment to one another, he wrote to George's father, painting me in a light as if I was a tainted lady. Mr. Davis, George's father, has been very plain about his intentions if George honors his engagement to me. George will be cut off completely, left absolutely penniless.

"And my uncle didn't stop there. He bullied Ivy's father into breaking off George and Ivy's betrothal and has refused to let George anywhere near the house."

I could finally see all of Eliza Mystery Wood. And oh, how I wished I could wake up and discover that it was all just a nightmare. I sensed that part of her was drawn to me as I was to her. I wanted to tell her it was me that she had kissed those nights ago. I wanted to tell her to choose me instead of Mr. Davis. But I knew it would only add to her troubled heart. She needed the man she already loved to help her—not me. And more than feeding my own selfish desires, I wanted Eliza's happiness.

I breathed out with regret. "Would Mr. Davis marry you now? Take you away from your uncle?" I hated the question, but it was necessary.

She nodded slowly. "He would. He has said he would do so the minute I say the word. But I have told him we must wait until he can reasonably find a way to support us. I don't know what we would live on. He has no skills to offer in the form of work, and although he had a good education, he is not one to apply himself. We would hardly be better off than beggars on the street."

"Miss Wood," I said, attempting a soothing tone. Protecting Eliza was my goal now.

She eventually looked up at me, uncertainty marking her eyes.

"I'll talk with Mr. Davis so we can secure your future." I took in a painful breath, then added, "And I'll not let you be sent away."

CHAPTER 12

Eliza Wood

January 5, 1817
Later that evening

I pressed the collar of Edward's coat to my nose and breathed in his scent once more as I sat on the edge of an old stained mattress atop a rusty metal frame. I rubbed my forehead, agitated. The sun had plummeted far below the horizon, and all was still and dark besides the moon, which sent a small beam of light across the floor. I had already pulled the pins from my hair to help with my pounding headache. I wasn't usually one for crying, but the last few days had provided a constant onslaught of one unexpected monstrosity after the next, beginning with kissing an unknown gentleman in the dark.

The worst part: It had gripped me so thoroughly that I hadn't even recognized it to be someone other than George until well into our second kiss. I touched my fingers to my lips at the memory, and my heart did an annoying flip. Unfortunately this kiss had consumed my thoughts on more than one occasion.

Technically the upheaval of my life had started two days prior to this all-consuming kiss. It had all begun on New Year's Eve after the Fortescue sisters had gone to bed. Sleep wouldn't come for me, so I had crept down the stairs to sneak one of the leftover biscuits from the evening's festivities. I was almost to the kitchen when I stopped hard in my tracks, hearing my uncle's voice, angry and raspy.

"I can't stand the sight of her any longer in my house," he growled.

"We've been over this a hundred times," my aunt's unfeeling voice said. "We promised." Her tone held no affection for me. Only duty and fear. She was a superstitious woman who believed in hauntings if one broke a promise to the dead.

"We have taken her in all these years," he retorted. "But she grows to look more and more like her mother with each passing day, and you know how I couldn't bear the sight of *her*. I won't stand to have her in my house."

My aunt scoffed. "You wouldn't mind so much if my sister hadn't refused your proposal all those years ago. And don't pretend to deny it. It's no secret I was not your first choice. Nor were you mine."

This was the first time I'd ever heard of such a thing. Imagining my uncle proposing to Mama or having any sort of tender feelings toward anyone was —impossible.

My uncle raged. "That's completely beside the point!" His voice shook. "I'll have her out of here if it's the last thing I do. I'll send her overseas, on one of those ships to America. Better yet, I could strap her to one of those merchant vessels. I'll not know where it takes her or whether the ship has been lost at sea. Or I could always send her to the workhouse." I could hear the cruel smile he was wearing as he painted each picture.

"I'll not send her away." My aunt's cold voice still held no emotion.

I was grateful to her all the same.

"But I know you will have what you want," she added with an unaffected tone.

"Indeed I will, if I haven't wrung her neck first," he said mirthlessly. "I will send her away immediately after the Fortescue brats' carriage departs," he spat.

"I know when I am beaten," she said without a morsel of sympathy for what these actions could possibly mean for me. "I wash my hands of it." Her words were as good as a death sentence.

My heart had pounded in my ears that night as their conversation came to a close. Fear overtook every part of my body as I quietly ran back to my bed and immediately started formulating a plan to escape my wretched fate. I would write to George—tell him of my dilemma. Surely he would think of something.

Yes.

I had quickly grabbed a piece of parchment and ink and began to write a coded message for him. I had planned to meet him at 10:30 in the farthest abandoned room from the south entrance of the ball that would be held in two days, where I would explain everything.

Two days later I kissed an unknown man— twice—instead of George. And instead of confessing my fears to George . . . I'd confessed them to—*him,* whoever he was.

If all that wasn't bad enough, I now held a secret. One, mind you, that I was trying my best to keep from myself.

My secret was this: A man I barely knew, Mr. Edward Livingston, had taken up most of my thoughts from the moment he'd held his ground and spoken his mind to my uncle at the ball the same night I kissed this unknown man. The dance we had shared was equally compelling. It was as if his vivid blue eyes could convey more than words ever could. And now, where George's eyes and easy smile used to be, I kept finding Mr. Livingston's instead. It plagued me with guilt and frustration.

And this afternoon, when Edward had pulled me close and looked into my soul, I thought he might kiss me. What's worse: I feared I might have let him if he'd tried. And now he was the only one who knew of my uncle's treacherous plans. I had confided in him before I had told another soul . . . unless you include—*him,* of course. The mysterious gentleman with lips that left me breathless . . . but I didn't include him.

What was wrong with me? I pulled my fingers through my hair and sank back on the bed.

I love George!

I had loved him for so long, though the hope of our love had been halted for a time.

I thought George would have fought harder for us when we were separated those years ago. But he had always been too kind to fight for anything.

He avoided conflict at all costs. And from the time we were separated, I had seen less and less of him.

I knew he still loved me. I saw it whenever he looked at me. I felt it in the few moments we were alone and he would embrace me. Or occasionally even kiss me.

This brought me to the other secret I was trying to keep from myself: Mr. Livingston's simple request to "examine" my hands, arms, and soul had made my heart trip more the last few days than all the kisses and embraces I had ever received from George combined.

No, I wasn't thinking about Edward! I was thinking about George. I let out an exasperated sigh.

I had also discovered that I had a great weakness: I was not very accomplished at keeping secrets from myself.

A sudden tapping sound came from my window, startling me. The corners of my lips lifted into a smile. It was George's signature move to throw rocks at my window at night, though his visits had been more scarce lately for fear that we would be discovered by my uncle. I shuddered, remembering the first time my uncle encountered us meeting in private.

Peeking out the window, I found his familiar eyes staring back, his kind smile in tow. He raised a hand and waved, and I waved back.

I quickly took off Mr. Livingston's coat, slid it beneath my bed, wrapped my shawl around my nightgown, and slid some boots on before I tiptoed down the stairs and out the back door.

George waited for me below and immediately embraced me when I came to him. His arms were familiar and welcoming—exactly what I needed to get Mr. Livingston out of my head. George then bent his face to mine and pressed a brief kiss to my lips.

I did not think of the gentleman I had kissed the other evening and the longing I'd felt from him.

No. I certainly did not.

I looked at George's kind eyes and let out a breath of relief that I could finally speak to him alone.

"How are you?" he asked with a sympathetic smile, as if he already knew I was in need of comforting.

I felt guilty for not thinking of him more these last few days. I also found myself frustrated that he had not come to me sooner at the party. My brows creased. "Why did you not meet me the other evening at the ball? Did you not receive my letter?"

He pulled away from me and gave a look of confusion. "I came only a few minutes after 10:30, but you were already gone. Why did you not wait for me?"

I could have slapped my face for the stupid question I'd just asked. It was, after all, I who had fled only minutes after arriving. He waited for my response, but I couldn't tell him what had happened.

I gave him an apologetic look. "You're right, I should have waited longer. I'm sorry. I was just unable to stay in that room any longer waiting for you."

It was technically the truth.

He gave me a look of understanding, then said, "I would have arrived early, but Ivy wanted to meet as well. She is worried about you. She told me that your uncle is acting strange. She worries that she may never see you again once she leaves with her sisters. Your letter seemed urgent. Liza, what is your uncle doing that has everyone so worried?"

I gave his hand a grateful squeeze, and then I told him everything about my uncle's plans.

CHAPTER 13

The sky slowly shifted to dawn, and with it came Edward's and my third and final plan for Ivy and Mr. Bentley to meet before the Fortescue sisters left for Lancashire this evening. My mind was heavy as I contemplated their departure. Ivy and her sisters were truly like family to me, and I was terrified to be without them.

As heavy as my mind was, if it allowed my heart to take over for only a minute, I found that it continued flipping over and over as I replayed Mr. Livingston's every touch, every look, as if it were all happening once again for the first time.

I had to give him up. I had to find a way to drive him from my mind. Today would be my last with Mr. Edward Livingston.

But when I neared the place where we usually watched Ivy and Mr. Bentley, I found a letter instead of the man who had been consuming my every thought.

It read:

My dear Miss Wood,

I regret that I am unable to meet you for our important mission this
     morning. I hope you will forgive my absence.
I have, however, delivered Mr. Bentley to his rightful place.
Your devoted friend,
Edward Livingston

My heart faltered as I read his message once, twice, three times. I felt the overwhelming urge to cry, which made me feel stupid. I had as good as told Mr. Livingston to leave me alone. And now I would never see him again. I looked at his elegant writing and traced my fingers over his words.

I hated that I felt so wanted—so alive—so safe in Mr. Livingston's company. George had said he would help me. He'd said he would marry me and do his best to support us both. None of it sat well with me. Not only would I be binding George to a life of poverty, but he would be bound to a woman whose heart was now split between two men. It felt dishonest. On top of it all, I didn't trust that George could actually protect either one of us from my uncle. He wasn't one to hold his ground or fight back.

I didn't even go to collect Ivy as I had the last two times. I didn't want to ruin her smile and rosy cheeks with my dismal mood. I walked in the opposite direction: the direction I always went when my uncle was unbearable and I needed a good bruising walk. It was a small journey that I could have walked with my lids shut tight.

My boots found the narrow gravel path that soon took me to a small trail between trees and fields. I let out a tense breath as I considered the plan that George and I had discussed. He would stand watch this evening until after the Fortescues left. I would sneak out of the house eventually, when the coast was clear, and George would have a chaperone waiting for me to take me somewhere safe.

At the time the plans were made, he hadn't a clue who that chaperone would be or where they would take me. My insides jittered just thinking about it. But what else was I to do? I could have left on my own, but I had nowhere to go.

My thoughts were interrupted when a snowflake melted on my cheek, followed by another. I looked up at the sky, and despite my melancholy mood, the corners of my mouth lifted. A snow-filled sky always took me to another world. A world filled with endless, soft white: a contrast to the hard darkness of my uncle's world. A snow-covered valley always left me with the dream of a different life.

I lifted my sleeve to examine the snowflakes collecting on my shawl. I was always determined to find two identical snowflakes, since it was said there were never two exactly alike. The intricate detail of each unique shard and crystal always made me marvel—

"Are you always so enchanted with a snow-filled sky?" A deep voice rumbled.

My hand flew to my heart, skipping at least two beats. But I knew that voice well, for I had been playing our conversations over and over in my mind.

I turned around to find Edward: back leaning against a tree, arms folded across his chest. He was not covered in white powder as I was, but looked absolutely perfect in his leisurely pose while dark, unruly curls fell over his forehead.

"How long have you been standing there watching me make a fool of myself?" I did my very best to sound severe, but a smile was already leaking through my words. I was so relieved to see him before I had to leave for—I couldn't finish the thought, since I didn't know where my departure would take me or if I'd ever see Mr. Livingston again.

He smiled at me, though it carried a heaviness. He stayed exactly where he was.

If I could have ripped out my traitorous heart and torn out the parts that longed for this man, I would have done so instantly. It would have made life far easier. As it stood, an ache formed in my chest as I realized I wanted him to come to me. And yet, he could never again wrap me in his arms or examine my hands—or soul. I would never discover his last request, which I was certain would have left me yearning for him even more.

He watched me, eyes guarded. "Is loving an enchanting sight so foolish?" His eyes moved to my snow-covered hair, my hands, now wrapping around my arms. His eyes then found mine. "If so, Miss Wood, I too am a fool." My heart pounded at the look he gave me, as if he wanted my nearness more than anything.

I took apprehensive steps toward him in order to take shelter. I stopped a few feet in front of him when he shook his head and a corner of his mouth twitched. "You still have that blasted thin shawl around your shoulders."

I opened my mouth with a smile and scoffed. "I couldn't exactly wear your coat Mr. Livingston, though I do think it looks better on me."

He tried not to grin but finally broke. "I can't argue with that."

"And it looks as though you have another coat," I pointed out.

"Yes, Miss Wood, I do have another coat. But the one you currently have in your possession is my favorite."

I gave him a look of mock pity then sighed as if we had a serious dilemma. "Perhaps we shall have to ask it which owner it wishes to remain with."

Edward's lips parted into a smile, and he chuckled. My heart beamed, as if I'd been waiting the whole day just to witness one laugh escape his mouth. It took everything in me not to take another step toward him. He, however, leaned away from the tree and took a small step toward me.

"Has George come to see you yet?" He studied my face. "I found him yesterday after you and I . . . talked." He forced his eyes away from mine and slowly put his hands inside his pockets. "I told him you were in trouble, and he said he had already been planning to speak with you that evening."

I nodded my head slowly and closed my eyes in dread at the reminder of my uncertain future.

"Thank you for taking the trouble to speak with George, Mr. Livingston. It was truly thoughtful."

After I related the plans George and I had discussed, he asked without emotion, "And when are you to be married?"

"We haven't decided," I said, barely above a whisper. "We both think it best for me to get settled first."

He nodded. "And where will you be staying until then?" His voice was ever so quiet.

"I haven't the faintest idea." Despite using a light tone, my voice shook. I sighed. "I will admit, Mr. Livingston, that I am nervous. I have no idea whom I will be meeting or where they will take me." My breath began to come out heavier until I began to shiver. Why was it that Mr. Livingston had this effect on me?

Stop shivering! I demanded to myself. But it was no use. Fighting the urge only made my teeth chatter harder.

Mr. Livingston watched me shiver with a tortured expression, then took his hands out of his pockets, reaching for me. I had only one thought at that moment. I needed him. I needed to feel his touch one last time. But just as his fingers grazed my arms, he froze, as if he was of two minds. He gave a slow exhale of frustration, then slowly withdrew his fingers and shoved his hands back inside his pockets. "Miss Wood," he finally said. "I know this may be the last time we see each other. But I must get you home so you—"

"Please don't say it," I whispered, stepping toward him and taking his hand in mine. I didn't know what possessed me to do it. I should have dropped his hand, but I clung to it instead, as if it were a lifeline, and held it near my heart. "This can't be goodbye," I said, feeling a desperation I couldn't fully understand.

Edward reached out once more with his other hand and brushed my cheek tenderly, as if he couldn't help it. My heart cried in longing with each touch. "Eliza, you are engaged," he whispered. I inwardly groaned at my actions as he reminded me, all while my stomach flipped at his use of my Christian name. "This must be goodbye," he breathed as he slowly raised my hand to his lips and pressed a soft kiss to it.

CHAPTER 14

We each shed tears as I gave a last hug to Ivy, Eleanor, Katherine, and Anne.

"Promise you'll write every day," Ivy cried, doing her best to put on a good face for me.

"Every day," I promised, wiping a tear from my own cheek. If only she knew what I was planning. But I didn't regret my decision to keep the information to myself. I couldn't have her worrying about me more than she already did.

The carriage was loaded too quickly, and then, without as much as a farewell from Uncle Fortescue or Aunt Margaret, the carriage pulled away.

I wrapped myself in Edward's coat like I had done each moment I was alone in my room. I breathed in the faint smell of sandalwood and soap that still lingered on the collar as I waited for the house to become still. I had made up my mind: I would take the coat with me until I was settled. Then I would find a way to send it back to Mr. Livingston.

Mr. Livingston.

How was I ever to get him out of my mind? I pressed my palms hard against my forehead and rubbed in case doing so might somehow erase Edward from my thoughts, until I heard the tapping at my window. I stopped rubbing my forehead.

That wasn't the plan, I thought to myself. Why was he throwing rocks?

My hands froze as I contemplated my next moves. Without making a sound, I left the bed and slipped on my boots. After buttoning Edward's coat, I quietly opened the door and crept down the hall toward the stairs.

But as I turned to descend the steps, I came face to face with Uncle Fortescue.

"THOUGHT YOU'D BE GETTING AWAY with it, didn't you?" He grabbed my arm and bared his teeth, holding a message in front of my face. My heart pounded as I tried to focus on the missive.

It was too dark to make out the details, but my pet name, "Liza" appeared at the top. George's name was signed at the bottom. My uncle must have intercepted it before it reached me. Dread filled every inch of my body.

"My dearest Liza," my uncle spat with a mocking tone, now pulling me down the stairs with him. I gasped back a sob and tried to pull away as he continued to read. "You will find me at your window once everything is ready to go." My uncle gave me a sinister grin and continued to pull me until we reached the last step. "Shall we go meet him then, *Liza?*" He growled as he said my name, then shoved me toward the door. "How much do you think Mr. Davis would like to talk with my fists again?"

My stomach turned as I recalled the last time my uncle's fists had found George. On that particular occasion two years ago, Uncle Fortescue wore pronged metal rings on each finger. Even now the tears came as I remembered it so vividly. With my uncle's first blow, the skin on George's jaw had split open from his jaw bone to just below his ear. George hadn't even tried to fight back. He was too good natured to use fists, and he still bore the scar of my uncle's rage.

A tear spilled out of the corner of my eye as my uncle showed me his fist. He bore his rings once more. "Please sir, that won't be necessary. You misunderstand its meaning," I cried, my voice little more than a whisper.

"Do you take me as a fool, you stupid girl?" he bellowed. "I'll not let you make a fool out of me!"

"No sir, I don't take you as a fool!" The fear in my voice was unmistakable, and I hated that he had this control over me. In that moment, I wanted to be brave. I wanted to stand up to my uncle the way Mr. Livingston had at the ball. I took a deep breath, and instead of cowering as he raised his fist to strike me, I stood my ground and raised my gaze to his black, soulless eyes and poured out every bit of judgment I could muster from my own.

"I take you as you are, Uncle," I said with venom, just as his fist was ready to strike. "A tyrant who will be haunted for the rest of his days by a woman he used to love."

My words shocked him long enough that he froze. I thought to pull away from him, but it would only have drawn him from his momentary trance.

"You think you are powerful because you will strike a lady or those who refuse to fight back." My voice shook. "You are despicable. And you will have to live with your despicable nature with no one to bully other than cold, heartless Aunt Margaret." I rallied my courage, then added, "I am leaving."

I pulled out of his grip and turned to leave. I didn't get two steps before his fingers dug into my arm and he spun me around.

"Oh, you'll be leaving alright," he growled. "But not with him." He gave me a cruel smile. "Once you're unconscious, you'll have nothing to say about the matter."

He raised his fist once more to strike me, and though I didn't flinch, I closed my eyes, awaiting my fate.

The front door burst open, a cold gust of wind hitting me suddenly. I gasped, eyes flying open. In his shock, my uncle released my arm. I tore away from him and spun around to warn George of the rings lining Uncle Fortescue's fingers. But it wasn't George who entered. It was—*him*. Edward. He wore a livid expression as he stared at my uncle, jaw set, unblinking.

Before I had time to do anything, Mr. Livingston took three swift strides toward me, took my hand, and pulled me behind him, shielding me from my uncle's wrath. Even from behind I could tell that Mr. Livingston's teeth were still gritted, eyes unyielding as they stared at my uncle.

"Meet me outside, Miss Wood," he said, barely able to control the anger in his voice. He let go of my hand so I could leave. I took a few steps away from Edward and went to the door. But I couldn't leave.

My uncle pierced me with a vengeful look. My heart caught in my lungs as he then pulled his fist back to strike Mr. Livingston. He was taller than Mr. Livingston and wider set. But before he struck, Mr. Livingston barreled his shoulder into my uncle's gut, taking him to the ground. My uncle staggered back but didn't completely lose his footing. He held his middle, though, as if the wind had been knocked out of him.

"I suggest you stay where you are, Mr. Fortescue," Edward seethed. He took a backwards step toward me to leave, but my uncle came after him at a run, ready to strike.

Edward dodged the first blow, but the second connected with his shoulder. He yelled out in pain and gritted his teeth, then blocked the next punch, returning a fist of his own right between the tyrant's eyes. My uncle staggered back, clutching his forehead. Mr. Livingston didn't ease backwards to leave this time. Instead, he immediately charged forward, taking my uncle to the ground.

I held my fingers over my mouth as Mr. Livingston quickly got to his knees and dealt a hard blow to my uncle's jaw as he attempted to find his feet. My uncle toppled back to the floor, lying flat on his back. Though a part of me still feared for Mr. Livingston, my heart swelled with gratitude and hope that not only was Edward willing to fight for my safety, but that he actually stood a chance against my uncle.

My uncle didn't attempt to get up again as Edward stood over him, then knelt, raising another fist, a look of disgust consuming him. For once I saw fear enter my uncle's eyes. But instead of striking, Mr. Livingston stopped short as my uncle flinched. Edward pounded his fist hard on the wood floor next to my uncle's ear like a gavel in a courtroom, making my uncle flinch once more.

Still kneeling, Edward clutched my uncle's lapels and forced his face upward so they were eye to eye. "How does it feel to cower, Mr. Fortescue?" Edward seethed. "Do you love feeling helpless?"

My uncle shut his eyes.

Mr. Livingston shook his lapels once more. "Look at Miss Wood," Edward demanded. My uncle refused until he was shaken once more. His eyes finally drifted to mine. I was surprised to find that I didn't find satisfaction in seeing him suffer. I did, however, find relief at knowing that we both knew he could be beaten.

"Now apologize," Edward said with unrelenting finality.

My uncle coughed then spat toward me. "I'll never apologize for doing something I don't regret."

Mr. Livingston shoved my uncle back to the ground, still holding his lapels, and hung over him, gritting his teeth. "Then let me make myself clear, Mr. Fortescue. Miss Wood is leaving your house tonight. If you try to stop her, or try to find her once she has left, I will find you. And next time I won't show mercy."

Edward forcefully let go of my uncle, then stood and turned toward me, scanning my face as if he feared he would find marks from my uncle's fists. The worried expression that marked his eyes softened as he walked toward me. He stopped just in front of the door and picked up a heap of fabric off the floor. He grinned as his eyes found the coat I had wrapped around my body. *His* coat.

His eyes met mine once more, and he leaned in to whisper so my uncle wouldn't hear. "Before you meet George, I wondered if we could speak privately for a brief moment out in the garden."

"Yes," I nodded, before leading the way.

CHAPTER 15

I found a secluded area that blocked us from the view of the house. Mr. Livingston stood directly in front of me, then spoke. "Other than acting as protector tonight, I have come to reclaim—this." He touched the fabric of the coat hanging below my hands.

The thought of giving up my one reminder of Mr. Livingston's warmth, comfort, and protection in the form of this coat was too much. I simply couldn't do it.

"I'm sorry sir, but it belongs to me now. You see, we understand one another." I tried to add a teasing tone to my voice, but the truth was that I didn't know if I had the courage to embark on the next part of my journey without a piece of him with me.

"Please, Miss Wood, I insist," he said, as if it weren't up for negotiation.

I gave him a look of pleading. "Can I send it to you later?" I looked back and forth between his eyes and bit my lip in hope. "Please?"

Edward unfolded the piece of fabric he was carrying and held it out in front of me. "I do believe this will fit you better for your journey," he grinned.

I opened my mouth as I stared at a lovely new lady's coat. "I couldn't possibly accept this from you, sir," I said, shaking my head. But a smile was leaking through at the thought that Edward had brought this to me.

He smirked. "And yet you feel no remorse about stealing my favorite coat?"

"But why is it your favorite?" I asked. "Your other coat appears newer. And it's more fashionable than this one."

Mr. Livingston considered my question before he said, "I must keep the answer of why it is my favorite to myself, Miss Wood." He studied my face for a moment. "But it is my final request."

I wrapped my arms around myself, breathing in the scent of his coat as it shifted.

"I will give it to you, Mr. Livingston, though it will be painful to do so." I looked up at him. "But I will only relinquish it once you've stated your reason for taking it from me."

Edward shook his head at my stubbornness, all while the corner of his mouth turned up ever so slightly.

"Why must *you* have my coat, Miss Wood?" he asked back in challenge.

But how could I answer his question? I couldn't exactly say, *"Well, Mr. Livingston, I do believe I'm falling in love with you, even though I've tried really hard not to. And this coat is the only thing I will have left of you once we are parted. I do believe that if you take it from me I will crumble."*

I looked at him and set my lips in a firm line. "I asked you first, Mr. Livingston." I folded my arms and cocked an eyebrow.

Edward exhaled in frustration and raked his hands through his curls. My eyes followed his fingers through the gesture, wondering what his hair would feel like between my fingers.

"Miss Wood," Edward finally said with desperation. "I am trying my hardest to be a gentleman." He dropped his hands and looked at me with a tortured expression. "If you have not discovered the way I long for you—the way my mind is consumed with images and thoughts of your eyes, your laugh, your voice, your smile—I would be astonished."

His words sent a wave of butterflies coursing through my heart before they rippled down into my stomach.

He didn't stop there. He took another small step toward me and breathed in slowly before he let it go in agony. "Do you have any idea how impossible it is to be near you without pulling you into my arms and holding you close?" He shook his head and looked at my lips. "How I long to kiss you?"

My heart exploded as he confessed the desires that had plagued my own mind. His breath came in and out as he looked at my eyes again.

His face leaned towards my ear. "You ask why I need this particular coat back," he said quietly.

My own breath moved rapidly as his breath grazed my neck.

"I need it back so that when I feel its warmth around me I can be sure that your warmth still exists somewhere, even if it's not intended for me. I need it back so I can envision you in it—and with that vision, the memory of your embrace. In short, Miss Wood, I need it back because when you leave, I can wear it and still have a small piece of you."

His every word mirrored my own feelings for needing this particular coat.

It was as if his entire being was made perfectly for mine, and I only needed to find myself in his company to discover it.

I glanced at Mr. Livingston. "It appears we both need it for the same reasons," I murmured.

The intensity of his eyes bored into my soul. He was seemingly gratified at my response, but torn.

"In that case, Miss Wood, I hesitantly admit that you must take it for now." He lifted his fingers toward my face as if he couldn't help it, then stopped as he was about to stroke my cheek.

He exhaled a tortured breath of frustration and lowered his fingers.

I hated myself. I wanted his touch so completely, yet my loyalty to George was years deep.

"I must go," Edward finally said, handing me the beautiful new coat. "I've already stayed too long. Mr. Davis will wonder where you've gone."

I nodded regretfully before Mr. Livingston took his leave, ensuring me that he'd continue to watch from a distance in case my uncle returned. Draping the new coat over my arm, I found George, as well as an elderly lady who would act as chaperone, standing below my bedroom window.

As George watched me approach, he gave me a questioning look as if he was trying to find my thoughts, then quickly replaced it with a shameful expression.

"Liza, I'm sorry I didn't intervene immediately. When I heard your uncle yelling, I was building up the courage to come inside and confront him. But then Mr. Livingston appeared. He must have been able to see my apprehension in facing your uncle. He told me to stay outside until everything was resolved. I am ashamed to admit that I was relieved. We both know I don't stand a chance against Mr. Fortescue in a fight."

George's words were not helping. Edward was the only person who had ever defended me against my uncle. And now—I looked at George. Would this man, the one who had claimed my affection for years, come to my aid if I needed it?

It was my last thought before George escorted my chaperone and me to a hidden carriage, awaiting our departure.

CHAPTER 16

January 13, 1817
One Week Later

It had been one week since I came to stay with Mrs. Groves, a widow in her 60s. She lived on the outskirts of Bath, where things were quiet. Despite the fact that I enjoyed her company, without the Fortescue sisters' games and stories I felt quite alone. Mrs. Groves and I mostly kept to ourselves, though we usually enjoyed meals and tea together. I found myself taking long walks to pass the time, though the weather was often dreary and sent me back inside. I appreciated that Mrs. Groves didn't hover. She also slept for a large part of the day and didn't mind if visitors called on me alone while she dozed—not that I received many. Only a few curious neighbors. I found myself painting or sketching more often than not while a restlessness grew inside me.

George had come by to see me only once in that time, and hadn't stayed very long. Something was different about him, and it made me feel even more alone. It was as if his eyes stated that he loved the sight of me more than ever, but at the same time he couldn't wait to be out of my presence. It made no sense.

I was in the middle of sketching when a knock came at the door. I hated that each time someone called, my heart hoped to see Mr. Livingston and his unruly curls enter the threshold. I was disappointed each time a neighbor of Mrs. Groves would appear instead, followed by guilt for not wanting it to be George first.

On this particular occasion, George did walk through the door, bringing me his usual smile. It was such a welcome sight.

"George!" I exclaimed, more excited to have company than I could explain. I threw my arms around him, sketchbook still in hand.

"Liza," he smiled as he gave me a squeeze. He chuckled as he realized I still clutched something in my fingers while giving him the biggest squeeze I could muster.

I gestured toward the sofa, and we both took a seat next to each other. I set my sketch pad on my lap and took his hand in mine.

"It is so good to see you." I smiled, grateful that he had finally come to keep me company.

There it was again. His smile dimmed as he looked down. He was aloof despite appearing as though he was truly happy to see me. An awkward silence hung between us for a moment.

"How are you settling in?" he asked with a kind smile, reminding me of why he'd first won my affection.

"Mrs. Groves has given me my own room that is not only comfortable, but beautiful as well. Thus far she has not raised a fist at me or raised her voice. Nor has she deprived me of any meals. Therefore, I must admit that other than being certain that I will die of boredom, I would be very ungrateful indeed if I didn't state that this arrangement is absolute perfection."

George smiled at my response. "I'm happy to hear it. And I *am* sorry you've been without my company these last few days."

"Where *have* you been?" I blurted before I could stop myself. I winced in embarrassment at my own prying, then added, "Forgive me, George. Of course you are busy. But I can't help but feel that something has happened that pulls you away from me. It's not as if you have an occupation that takes up your time."

A thought suddenly hit me that I had never considered. What if George had fallen in love with someone else? What if it had snuck up on him the way it had for me and Edward?

"George?" I asked, taking his hand tentatively. "Has another woman won your affection?"

George breathed out an ironic laugh then looked at me solemnly. "I believe it is the other way around." He picked up my sketch pad and glanced at it briefly before turning it around to face me. Mr. Livingston's eyes stared back, a look of intensity marking his expression. George set it aside, then looked at me expectantly.

My throat tightened. "What do you mean?" I asked, dreading his response.

He looked at me with sympathy. "I'm not angry with you, Liza. The heart isn't something we can always control. And Mr. Livingston has protected you and reached a part of you that I don't even know how to begin to reach. But the realization doesn't hurt any less regardless of what you or I do at this point."

"I love *you*, George," I reassured him.

"I know you do." He gave me a sad smile. "But I have never seen you look at me the way you did Mr. Livingston when I came upon you the other day in the snowy woods."

I opened my mouth to explain, but he put up a hand. My pulse quickly picked up speed, pounding so loudly that I could hear it.

My vision blurred as I looked at his knowing expression until a tear finally escaped. How could I have let this happen?

"I recognize your loyalty to me, Liza. And I know there is a part of you that loves me dearly. But I wonder if it is enough." He gently brushed the tear that trailed down my cheek, then continued. "My heart has always belonged to you, and I will do anything you ask." He paused. "But Liza, I can't help but feel that eventually we would despise our decision if we were to be married. A penniless life is hard enough. I believe it would be even more impossible for us both if your heart were not mine alone."

I wanted to protest—to tell him that I would forget Edward Livingston. But George was right. And if I stared at the truth long enough, it would tell me that if I stopped pushing away my feelings for Edward, he would steal my heart entirely.

More than that, if George and I didn't marry, I could release him from living a penniless life. Though it should have been easy to give him up for that reason alone, I was selfish. The idea of losing George was, in truth, terrifying.

He'd been a constant solace to me from the time I'd lost my parents. I would miss his easy smile and temperament, his kindness and goodness. But George deserved better than that. We both did.

I looked up at him and smiled through my tears. "I could not have lived without your kindness and love all these years." I took his hand in mine once again, and though I could see the pain in his eyes, there was also something else. They spoke of hope for a future without poverty, of finding a fresh love once more. "I wish you all the happiness in the world, Mr. Davis." I swallowed down the fear that twisted in my gut as the finality of those words sank in.

George laid his hand over our entwined fingers, then leaned in and kissed my cheek. "And I wish *you* all the happiness in the world, my dear Liza."

He didn't stay to visit or for tea. He gave me a reassuring look and a hopeful smile, lined with heartache, then left without looking back.

I stayed in my room for the remainder of the day. Despite the fact that George was right, and we were better off going our separate ways, I cried myself to sleep.

CHAPTER 17

The next three days hadn't brought either sunshine or the serenity of snowfall to cheer up my lonely heart. It brought only bouts of rain and a dark grey sky until day slowly shifted to evening.

I sat on the window seat in Mrs. Groves's small library and stared at the garden, now dormant and wilted. I hugged Mr. Livingston's coat to my heart and breathed in the scent that was beginning to fade as I leaned back on some decorative pillows situated against the wall of a small alcove. I worried that Edward had forgotten me, and just like his scent, would slowly fade until he was real only in my mind. I glanced over at the sketch I had been working on and let out a groan. Most of my sketches lately were of—*him*.

Penciled-in eyes stared back at me in the dim light, and I found that I wanted to crumple the piece of parchment into a ball and throw it into the low-burning fire. No matter how well I remembered him, I could never draw his features exactly right.

Eventually my eyes turned heavy until they closed completely and I drifted to sleep.

~

THE FAINT CREAK of the library door startled me awake. When I opened my eyes, a small beam of light spilled onto the floor from the open door. A figure entered, carrying a candle, but my eyes were still blurry from sleep.

"Is that you, Mrs. Groves?" I asked, blinking in the dim light. Whoever it was, their back now faced me as the door handle clicked shut.

"Mrs. Groves has asked me to collect you." It was *his* deep voice that echoed in the quiet space, making my heart jump out of my chest.

My breath sped up as the figure turned to face me. And as I stared at his eyes flickering in the candlelight, I knew once and for all I would never be able to sketch them perfectly.

Those same compelling eyes moved to where I lay on the window seat, and he gave me a smile as if he found it all amusing. I quickly stood and straightened my dress, grateful for the darkness so he couldn't see the shameful blush that now marked my cheeks.

I didn't know whether to smile or cry at seeing him so unexpectedly. And now he was seeing me in my day dress wrinkled from sleep. If I'd known he was coming, I would have taken extra time with my hair and worn my loveliest evening gown.

A flare of embarrassment hit me, and my words came out clipped. "And what do you find so amusing, sir?" I raised an eyebrow of challenge. "Have you never fallen asleep somewhere other than your bed?"

He tried to bite back a grin but wasn't equal to the task. "As a matter of fact, Miss Wood, I make a habit of dozing wherever I please." His smile grew. "I only find it ironic that our roles seem to have reversed from our first meeting."

My forehead creased, not understanding his veiled meaning. Was it perhaps some sort of metaphor?

"Our first meeting? I don't follow you, Mr. Livingston," I said.

He placed his candle on a small table, then stepped close to me, his hand brushing against my arm. His eyes consumed me; I was sure I would drown in their depths and never resurface.

"Perhaps I can show you," he said in a low, simmering voice.

He waited for a moment, as if he wanted to make absolutely sure I didn't object. My breath picked up speed as he gently moved his fingers around mine in the darkness and eased my hands up until they rested on his chest. My pulse was on fire. He slowly wrapped his arms around me and pulled me in until I rested against him. His heart beat fast and strong, mirroring my own. I leaned into him and breathed out a sigh of longing as he held me close. His every breath, every heartbeat spoke louder than any words ever could. He needed me, just as I needed him. As we stood in the quiet, my entire being reveling in the feel of him close to me, I didn't care that his memory was serving him wrong. Nevertheless, I still had to correct him.

"You remember this as our first meeting?" I smiled, remembering the day he'd requested to help warm up my shivering arms. I leaned the side of my face against his chest and wrapped my arms around his back, easing myself even closer. "If memory serves me well, it certainly wasn't our first meeting, but perhaps it was our third."

"Or perhaps," he whispered in my ear, sending tingles down my neck and straight to my heart, "*you're* remembering incorrectly." My head swam from his nearness, making it impossible to think clearly. "Since you denied my request to keep my coat," he grinned with a low husky voice, lips almost touching my ear, "my last request is to test your heart." My breath hitched as he tenderly brushed his lips against my cheek. He moved his fingers to caress my face, then slowly guided my lips towards his. "Do you accept my last request?" he whispered as his eyes found my lips. He let his request sink in as our lips remained a breath apart.

My heart thudded as his lips drew me in. I had wanted this for what felt like ages. I laced my fingers around his neck and eased his lips to mine. Our lips moved slowly against each other while my heart burned. My fingers caressed the side of his face, then slowly moved to the back of his hair. As I shut my eyes and tasted Edward's lips, the feel of his hair between my fingers, another memory began to take shape, merging with this one. A dark room nights ago, and a kiss of longing shared by two strangers. A kiss that consumed the mind and soul. I pulled my lips away from his, a small gasp escaping me. I understood what Edward was trying to show me.

"Our first meeting," I whispered, my breath coming in and out in heavy waves from his kiss. "It was—*you*—" I stammered. "You were—"

My head swam. I couldn't decide if I felt enchanted or fooled by the realization.

"How long have you known?" I asked, deciding I felt betrayed. I moved my fingers away from his hair, hoping he hadn't been playing some kind of game with me.

"Eliza." His deep voice came out quiet and sincere. I hated that a whispering current of tingles and warmth spread down my spine at hearing my Christian name uttered by him. He looked back and forth between my eyes in the dim light. "I only discovered the truth when examining your soul."

His eyes begged me to believe him as I tensed.

He exhaled, then asked, "Will you please let me explain?"

Although I was afraid of what I might find from his explanation, I needed answers.

I breathed out with trepidation, then nodded once for him to proceed.

He raked a hand through his hair. "Where to begin?" he said as he looked at me. "You asked if I have never fallen asleep somewhere other than my bed." His lips turned up into an ironic grin. "Until we shared that first all-consuming kiss, I was determined to spend my time alone, preferably napping, in the darkest, emptiest room of every party and ball, to ensure that I remained an unmarried gentleman for the remainder of my days. I had retired from the ballroom with a headache and chose the coldest, darkest room I could find." He chuckled. "I was intending to take a nap when you opened that blasted door. The first time I opened my mouth to tell you who I was, you took my hand, rendering me speechless."

I thought back to the day Edward examined my hands and the way it had done something similar to me.

"And then, my dear Eliza," he said, one side of his lips turning up, "you did the unthinkable and kissed a man who was already having an impossible time completing a full sentence. Unfortunately, though I still can't bring myself to regret my actions, I had no idea what sort of spell your lips would cast over my good judgment. After you kissed me, I finally found the words to say. But I found that I no longer wanted to say them. I was so moved by your heart—your sincerity, your longing. I was driven mad by that kiss, not knowing who you were or what you looked like."

I understood his sentiment, for I, too, had wondered whose face belonged to such a kiss. Though at the time, I had mostly felt guilt at not realizing it hadn't been George. And I had felt so disoriented after discovering the fact that I'd been kissing a stranger that I hadn't focused on the sound of his voice when he asked me to wait.

Edward continued to explain that he originally thought Ivy had been the stranger he had kissed. That he'd intended to find out more about her and had even considered winning over her heart.

He raised his fingers to my cheek and lightly stroked my skin. "Then I met you," he said, eyes simmering. "I was drawn to you so easily and I found myself relieved, thinking you were not my mystery lady. *She* was, after all, in love with somebody else."

The back of Edward's fingers traced down my neck, leaving me breathless before he said, "But Eliza Wood's heart was free, as far as I knew. She felt so perfect in my arms and had no uncle that I was aware of."

He took my hand in his once more, then gently brought his other fingers beneath my face and slowly raised my chin until I was looking into his eyes. "So I fell for Miss Eliza Wood instead, intent on winning her heart completely." His eyes bore into the deepest recesses of my soul, and his next words came out just above a whisper. "Until I searched her soul and discovered that she did indeed have an uncle. And that her heart already belonged to someone else."

I closed my eyes in understanding as my heart confirmed the truth of his words.

"Eliza," he whispered, brushing the top of my hand with his fingers. "I wanted to tell you everything the night I discovered the truth. I wanted to persuade you to love me instead of Mr. Davis. I wanted to kiss you again to prove why you should be with me."

My heart hammered as he admitted these words, and I couldn't help but raise my hand to the side of his face and trail my fingers through his hair.

He closed his eyes at my touch and leaned his head against my hand before he opened his eyes once more.

"But it was a selfish desire," he said. "And more than wanting you for myself, I wanted your safety and happiness. I wanted you to have what you needed. So I kept the secret buried, believing I would carry it forever."

I could no longer feel betrayed. My only desire now was to end our anguish.

His eyes dropped to my lips. "But it is rumored that your heart is now free to choose." The hunger in his eyes was unmistakable and made my stomach flip.

"It is," I breathed, slowly lifting my other hand to his back, then gliding my fingers over his neck and up the back of his hair.

He exhaled in relief and pleasure, then brought my lips close, making my heart trip.

"And what does your heart say about me?" he whispered before his lips slowly lowered to mine, kissing me tenderly. His movements were sweet caresses, stealing every inch of my heart. I felt the urge to cry for the way I felt his heart cling to mine. His lips were deliberate and ached of longing, leaving me breathless.

I relished the feel of his unruly curls between my fingers. His arm wound around me, and he pulled me close as his lips continued to discover mine. His kiss turned achingly tender before he moved his lips to my ear.

"Eliza," he breathed, taking one of my hands from his hair and pressing it to his heart. His breath came in and out quickly. "Please tell me you feel for me the way I feel for you." Our eyes met, and he was wearing his heart out in the open while it pounded beneath my fingers.

Did he not know that every beat of my heart called out for him? I moved my other fingers from his hair to his cheek. "My heart says that I have been consumed with thoughts of you since our first meeting—that I crave to be near you and to know your thoughts. It tells me that perhaps your soul was made for mine and I simply had to find you in order to recognize it."

As I spoke the words aloud, I knew them to be true. George had made me happy, and we would have been happy together if I had never met Mr. Livingston. But Edward's soul spoke to mine in a way no one's ever had.

Edward's eyes filled with satisfaction at my words, and he pressed another soft kiss to my lips before he said, "Then I have one final request."

"I believe I'm inclined to accept it," I grinned, already knowing that I would like whatever it was that he requested.

"May I test your heart every day?" His fingers trailed down my arms and ended at the tips of my fingers. "Because I'm not done examining your hands."

He kissed my fingers. "Or warming your arms." He began easing my arms around his back, though it was unnecessary. My arms were already on their way around him, pulling myself close.

He tucked my hair behind my ear as he looked into my eyes. "I will certainly need your soul every day—your thoughts, your laughter, and even your sorrow. I want to share it all with you."

My heart was bursting. I wasn't surprised when a tear ran down my cheek. "Do you promise to test my heart every day?" I smirked, watching his lips turn up.

"Every—single—day," he said as he kissed me again, taking every measure to ensure that he thoroughly—kept—his promise.

Another tear trailed down my cheek, and when our lips parted, I couldn't help but smile in sheer joy. Only two words remained unspoken—two words that would taste sweeter than any words I'd ever uttered before.

"I accept."

THE END

ACKNOWLEDGMENTS

A big thank you to my editors, Ruth Owen and Ashlyn Pells, for making this possible, and to my husband for mentioning the idea for this book in passing and then helping me in the beginning stages to figure out who Edward Livingston should be. And as always, thank you to my sweet girls, who are so patient while I write, and who cheer me on.

ABOUT THE AUTHOR

Jana L. Perkins is a romance writer who is devoted to giving her readers a sweeping experience that leaves them wanting more. A mother of three, Jana homeschools her daughters. She believes that education is essential for every mind, young and old, and should be explored in many different ways. When Jana isn't writing or teaching her children, she enjoys taking long walks with her husband, playing with her dogs, and trying new things.

For more books and updates, visit https://www.thecrimsonarchives.com/.

Printed in Great Britain
by Amazon

59390308R00059